TWO FACES OF THE JAGUAR

GEORGE DISMUKES

TWO FACES OF THE JAGUAR
Copyright © 2020 George Dismukes

ISBN: 978-1-68046-897-7

Melange Books, LLC
White Bear Lake, MN 55110
www.melange-books.com

Published in the United States of America.

Cover Design by Ashley Redbird Designs

To Nadine

NOTE FROM THE AUTHOR

All geographic locations referenced in *Two Faces of the Jaguar* actually exist. This includes The Lost City of The Monkey God, which lies in the far eastern "Gracias A Dios" section of The Mosquitia Jungle in Honduras. I only renamed one place, the village of Sambala is actually called Sambo Creek.

Honduras is a Latin country and the national language is Spanish. Although many of the characters in this story are American, just as many are Honduran. In a natural environment, many of the conversations might have taken place in Spanish. But that would make the story distracting in the least, and to most, likely unreadable Therefore, we have left only a few throw-away comments and expletives in Spanish.

The characters are all fictitious, but most of them are extracts of people I have known. Andrea Granger is a composite.

CHAPTER ONE

Bad Dawn in Sambala

DAWN BROKE PEACEFULLY ALONG THE NORTH COAST OF Honduras. Small waves washed up onto a coral sand beach as if it were too much trouble to make the effort. The fronds of coconut palms barely swayed, slowly, gracefully, to and fro. Small fiddler crabs scurried about on the sand, outrunning each incoming wave. The coastal village of Sambala, nestled against the Caribbean Sea, slept.

That is, most of it. There was one exception to this pastoral scene. On a narrow dirt backstreet of Sambala existed a rectangular clapboard building painted dark blue with a rusting tin roof. The building rested on round pilings which suspended its floor five feet above the ground. A large half-moon shaped cement stairway and landing gave the building entrance a much grander entrada than it deserved.

It was the activity going on inside this structure which gave the whole place a sinister aura. The interior was designed like a primitive sanctuary. Two rows of pews lined each side with a center aisle leading to a dais at the back end of the building. Animal skulls were tied to the wooden pole rafters. Voodoo figurines made of corn husks and straw festooned the walls here and there.

A podium stood atop the dais, and adjacent to that, an iron barred cage, four feet wide by six feet long and four feet tall. A two-hundred-pound jaguar lay inside the cage. She was black as night, and her name was Naja. She was, much to her dismay, the instrument of this temple's leader; a man who had the gall to call himself, "Smoke Jaguar." That's what he called himself, a royal name usurped from an ancient Mayan king of Copan.

Nobody knew his real name, and his origin was equally vague. He spoke with an accent that hinted of Jamaica. But he had never admitted to it. He was tall, thin, sported a shaved head, but not a shaved face. He wore, dark sunglasses, even when indoors, and dressed in an off-white muslin robe which fell to the top of his sandaled feet.

He stood behind the podium, adjacent to the iron cage, ranting like a madman. Most of his words were incoherent to all except him. Occasionally he would bring down a heavy walking stick hard on top of the cage, which infuriated Naja and elicited a furious roar from her every time. The thunderous sound within the small building had managed to reawaken those with the temerity to doze during Smoke Jaguar's rambling diatribe.

Sitting on the second row of pews to the left side of the building was an exhausted Amer-Indian woman named Anna Maria, and her six-year-old son, Evaristo. Anna Maria cared less about what Smoke Jaguar was saying, even if she would have been able to understand him, which she couldn't.

She sat there because her drunkard husband had staggered home from one of the palapa bars on the beach at about 2:00 a.m. He was higher than a Ceiba tree and in a romantic mood. After pawing her breasts way too roughly, and then demanding that she service him orally, she railed against his demands, grabbed her child and escaped out the front door.

She wandered aimlessly through the back streets of Sambala for an hour. Then, when she could walk no more, she spotted the open doors of the temple and wandered in simply because it offered a place to sit. She was so tired that she was even willing to put up with the nonsensical spewing of Smoke Jaguar. At least he wouldn't be trying to run his hand up her skirt and force his fingers inside her.

Now, in slumber, Anna Maria became oblivious to all sights and sounds around her. Sleep took her blissfully away from her misery. Evaristo, on the other hand, was left to his own devices. He had napped, but the miracle of youth permitted him to awaken refreshed after an hour.

In 'forma de six,' he was curious, and enthralled by the majestic black cat in the cage.

No one noticed when Evaristo abandoned his mother's side and made his way around the end of the pew. Like Anna Maria, what few visitors there were to the Temple of The Black Jaguar were asleep, even in the face of non-stop jabbering.

Little Evaristo approached the dais and stood in front of the cage watching the huge cat from scant inches away. Naja saw the child, but he represented no threat to her, so she dismissed his presence and laid her head on her paws. Evaristo, on the other hand, couldn't understand why she didn't roar at him.

After watching for several uneventful minutes, Evaristo reached over and seized the large walking stick from where it rested against the side of the cage. Heavy in his small hands, Evaristo didn't possess the size or strength to bang it down on top of the cage. Instead, he slipped one end of it through the bars and jabbed as hard as he could at the ribs of Naja.

Like everyone else present in the temple, with the possible

exception of Smoke Jaguar, Naja felt exhausted. Because Smoke Jaguar had left her alone for a while, she dozed. But the shock of a foreign object being jammed into her side awoke her in surprise and fury. She roared loudly and sprang backward to try and escape the invading object. In so doing she set two things into motion.

(1) The offending stick cantilevered between the bars of the cage. The large end of the stick was below Evaristo's arm. The force of the stick now launched him, flinging him through the air like some child's doll. He landed hard against the wall of the building. The impact knocked him unconscious and he slumped to the floor.

(2) When she sprang backwards, trying to escape the stick, Naja's flank hit hard against the old rusty door of the cage. It was as if providence itself intervened, when horrifyingly, the latch gave way and the door creaked slowly open. The event got Smoke Jaguar's immediate attention and caused him to finally shut up. He turned his attention to the cage. Seeing the door swing open, and seeing Naja turn toward that door, the seemingly fearless Smoke Jaguar started to panic. His eyes grew wide with fear.

Meanwhile, when Naja realized what had happened, she turned toward the door and moved to it slowly, cautiously. It was at this precise moment that Smoke Jaguar gave in to his fear. He screamed a blood curdling alarm, jumped down from the dais and scrambled toward the front of the building, pausing only a moment to grab a straw basket sitting on a small table, containing several bills of money.

The terrified attendees, including Anna Maria, followed him, having been roused by the ruckus, to say nothing of Smoke Jaguar's horrific scream. Men and women poured out the front of the building, down the steps and onto the dirt street. Smoke Jaguar slammed the old wooden double doors shut and tied them with a rope which fit through holes where knobs would normally be.

He then had the presence of mind to call for assistance from some of the male followers. He told them to go quickly on both sides of the building and close the wooden shutters which were hinged at the top and held open by prop sticks. Several men responded with surprising alacrity and speed. Within moments, they secured the building. The mayhem was contained, but now what? Smoke Jaguar's mind raced. "What next?" He wasn't sure.

He leaned back against the double doors, clutching his straw basket of money tight against his chest. He had fucked up badly, and he knew it. He needed time to think. His narcissistic mind was already seeking remedies for this mess. How could he get out of this with minimal damage control?

The first issue was, of course, the little problem of a three-hundred-pound jaguar loose inside his temple. Naja did not like him, so it wasn't as if he was going to be able to go in there and call to her by saying, "Here kitty-kitty!" Given the chance, she would use her razor claws to turn him into thick sliced bacon.

Dawn was bringing light to Sambala. The sun peeked over the horizon. Now that Anna Maria spent a few moments waking up and gathering her thoughts, she began looking for Evaristo. She didn't see him, so she called to him. Then, the horrible truth hit her. Evaristo was still inside the temple... with the black jaguar!

Horrible confirmation of Anna Maria's fears came a moment later. Naja roared so loudly that the building vibrated. At the same time, Evaristo screamed a prolonged, terrified scream. After that, only a deafening silence came from inside the temple.

Witnesses surrounding the front of the building had heard it all. Their eyes grew wide in disbelief and horror. Anna

Maria went into shock. She had heard her child's scream. She tried to hold her arms out, but they felt like lead. She sagged down onto the concrete steps, held her face in her hands and began to sob.

There was one person present at the gathering whom no one had noticed. He had been passing by en route to his morning errands when the stampede out the front doors of the temple drew his attention. His name was Julio. He was fifteen, born and raised in Sambala. He was skinny, burned dark brown by the Central American sun, a thick mass of hair on his head. He was an intelligent lad and it only took him a moment to size up the severity of the situation.

He knew for sure there was only one person alive who could defuse this situation. He needed to run fast and find Brandon Shaw. There was not a moment to lose if wholesale bloodshed was to be averted in his village. Julio turned toward Cuyamel and ran like the wind.

CHAPTER TWO

Unexpected Surprise

THE OLD, FADED BLUE, FLATBED TRUCK WITH WOODEN SIDERAILS groaned with every move as it made its way slowly along the pothole filled road. Calling it a road was being gratuitous; it hardly qualified for the term. In truth, it was no more than a wide bulldozed path through the jungle which ran parallel with the north coast of Honduras. The road was re-graded every couple of months to keep it passable, not that it did much good. On the day of the grading, it looked reasonably flat, but the moment a rain came, which was often, potholes reappeared like magic, turning the road into a pockmarked nightmare. There was no way to dodge one hole without hitting another. If one had enough patience and most of all, endurance, they could travel the road as far east as the edge of the Mosquitia jungle.

The truck was pointed west, coming from a business called Jungle Cargo at Cuyamel, on the beach, destination, the airport at La Ceiba. The side rails clattered as they rocked back and forth with each bump. The live cargo, in shipping crates on board the truck screamed their disapproval to no avail. Monkeys, various species of birds, tayras, agoutis, kinkachoos, jaguarundis, coati mundis, and beneath all those crates, the flat wooden boxes with tiny holes drilled in the sides. Boxes filled with venom wielding deadly vipers, snakes; fer-de-lance, tropical rattlesnakes, jumping vipers, things no person in their right mind would come within a hundred yards of. But to Brandon Shaw, it was all in a day's work. For him, the snakes held no dread. They were his stock-in-trade. What did hold dread for him this morning was the pothole dotted road.

At the moment, he sat slumped on the passenger side of the bench seat, clinging to the window frame for additional support. Lorenzo Ponce, his young Amer-Indian right-hand man drove the truck. Lorenzo was slight, dark skinned with a perpetual smile.

As the truck sank into another jolting hole, Brandon cursed under his breath and held his aching head.

"Jesus Christ, Lorenzo! The object is to try and miss a hole every now and then; not try to run up a score by hitting as many as possible."

Lorenzo wrestled with the large steering wheel and laughed at his boss. "Maybe if you hadn't tried to drink all the rum in Cuyamel last night, your crudo might not be so bad this morning!" Lorenzo chided in his thick, Honduran accent. The truck sank into another pothole with a wrenching toss to the left.

"Yeah. Thanks for the sage advice," Brandon said with sarcasm.

The thick, coastal jungle crowded right up to the road. Tree branches scraped against the truck constantly. It created the illusion of traveling through a green tunnel. Adding to the adventure, there were three small streams that had to be forded en route to town. Normally, each one was no more than fifty feet from bank to bank, and a few inches deep. But it was the beginning of the rainy season in Honduras.

A mountain range was set back from the coast less than

half a mile in some places. When it rained, water cascaded down from the slopes and swelled the small streams to dangerous levels. Traffic, such as it was, frequently stalled for hours following a downpour, waiting for the water level in the streams to abate enough to allow passage. But the day was still young and most of the rains boiled up in the afternoons in response to the heat.

As they pushed on through the green tunnel en route to La Ceiba, Lorenzo did his best to avert as many potholes as possible, although, missing them all was impossible. The slamming sound of a tire sinking into a hole was so frequent and consistent that it almost established a rhythm.

More than an hour passed before the green tunnel widened and then gave way completely to signs of civilization. The truck and all its occupants had arrived at the outskirts of La Ceiba. A blacktop road now stretched out before them. With one final bump, the truck launched itself up onto the blacktop and left the pot holed nightmare behind. Both passengers in the truck sighed with relief, and the terrified screaming from the cargo area diminished.

They had traveled less than half a mile, however, when Brandon pointed at a blue, cinderblock building on the left side of the road and said, "Pull in there."

The parking lot fronting the building was not paved. Therefore, once again, they left the blacktop with a bump and rolled to a stop in front of the "Gato Azul," a cantina, identified by a not so well drawn blue cat over the frieze of the door. The words "Gato Azul" were painted above the cat in the shape of an arch.

Two screen doors secured the front opening of the Gato Azul. The doors managed to keep the flies from getting out more than getting in. Brandon climbed down from the truck slowly, in pain not only from his hangover, but the ride to town.

With both feet on the ground, he turned to Lorenzo and asked, "Anything to drink?"

"Si," Lorenzo said loudly, over the sound of the truck, "Una soda naranja, por favor."

"Orange soda!" Brandon repeated. "Okay!"

Brandon opened one of the screen doors and entered the half dark enclosure. There were several metal tables scattered around the rough, uneven concrete floor. The air smelled of stale beer and cigarette smoke. Most of the place replicated any typical Central American bar. But the actual bar within the barroom was as out of place as a diamond in a homeless shelter.

The massive, dark stained mahogany wooden structure stood four feet tall, with hand carved reliefs of Mayan scenes, copies from archaeological sites, inlaid from one end of the bar to the other. Centrally positioned on the bar front was a depiction of a Maya chieftain, adorned in war regalia, a jaguar pelt over the shoulders, a huge bonnet of Quetzal feathers, standing with one foot on the back of a supine captive.

It was impossible to see this magnificent work of art without wondering how the hell it came to be here, in this dump. The owner must have appropriated it from some hotel that went defunct. That, or there had to be some other really good story about how the expensive work wound up here.

Brandon paused a moment to admire the depictions before approaching. A squat looking Amer-Indian woman stood behind the bar with a blank expression on her face.

"Buenos dias!" Brandon greeted.

"Buenos dias!" the woman replied.

"I need six beers to go," he said. "Oh, and one orange soda." The woman opened a large cooler behind the bar and removed the beers, setting the wet bottles on top of the bar-top which showed damage from constant similar abuse.

Brandon could not help shaking his head slightly and

saying, "Pearls before swine!" If only he had room for this thing, he would offer the owner whatever he wanted for it, just to rescue it from exposure to peons and uncaring, constant abuse.

"Please open one of them," Brandon said. The woman complied, and Brandon turned the bottle up until it was drained. He replaced the empty on the bar, belched and said, "Open one more, please."

The woman complied, again. She placed the other bottles, including the orange soda, in a plastic bag. Brandon tossed money on the bar, thanked her, took his purchase and retreated to the front door.

Outside, Lorenzo waited patiently, truck motor idling. By now, the air around the truck was pungent with the smell of gasoline fumes. Brandon climbed into the truck, withdrew Lorenzo's soda pop and handed it to him. They kept an opener in the unused ashtray. Lorenzo lifted the cap off his drink, took a deep sip, and turned the truck back toward the road. They bounced back onto the blacktop and turned left, toward town and the airport.

Brandon opened one beer after another, gulping down the contents until finally the pain between his ears began to abate. Lorenzo ignored him, focusing instead on his driving. Oddly, he was much more at home driving on the pothole filled road. He was a country boy, having been raised in the village of Sambala. City traffic spooked him. So many people, so many cars, so many ox carts clogging traffic with their heavy loads of papaya, plantains and mango.

This was to say nothing of the naïve Indians walking the streets who had been forced to come to town for one reason or another. They understood nothing at all about city traffic and constantly walked out in front of moving vehicles. Why more of them weren't injured or killed was a wonder. One had to constantly be on alert for them, and this old truck didn't exactly stop on a dime.

Twenty minutes later they turned right off the main road onto the airport access. The terminal was less than five minutes away. As they approached, Lorenzo turned into a short drive adjacent to the terminal and came to a stop in front of a hurricane fence gate. A uniformed officer came out of a guard house and opened the gate for him. Lorenzo would have, under normal circumstances, been required to let the guard inspect his export documents. But the guard and Lorenzo had been through this same routine so many times over the years that the inspection routine had long since been abandoned.

Instead, there was usually some kind of a gift proffered, which also prevented seizure of any animals that might be on the protected species list. Today, the gift was a small white envelope, discreetly handed to the guard as he approached the truck to greet Lorenzo. The guard tipped his hat and waved the truck through.

The company's old DC-6, gutted and re-fitted to carry animal crates waited on the tarmac. At this point, Brandon split off from Lorenzo. Lorenzo's next job was to do what he had done so many times in the past that he could do it in his sleep.

He off-loaded all the incoming supplies from the plane and set the boxes on the tarmac. Next, he began transferring crates from the truck, onto the plane.

Large fans were set up at the bay doors to keep air circulating through the aircraft until takeoff time. Extra workers appeared for these tasks. When the truck was empty, the incoming supplies would be loaded on board.

While these operations were taking place, Brandon made his way inside the terminal to find his partner, Doug Bennet. Brandon found him in the same place where he usually found him, at the customs desk.

But this time there was a surprise. Doug was not alone. A long-haired blond woman accompanied him. She seemed too beautiful to be here, somehow out of place in these environs.

Be that as it may, Brandon leaned against a close at hand marble column and listened as she spoke to the customs officer in impeccable Spanish. Doug looked almost sheepish standing next to her. At one point, Doug turned, spotted Brandon, and waved to him. Brandon waved back with a half-smile. Like Brandon, Doug was attired in a khaki safari outfit. But that's where the similarity ended. Brandon was tall. Doug Bennet was barely five-eight. Brandon walked with a swagger. Doug walked in measured steps. And he had a slight speech impediment. He frequently repeated words or sentences when he spoke.

It didn't take long until the customs agent, obviously charmed by the beautiful blonde, stamped the visas in their passports and wished them a pleasant stay. Then they turned and walked toward Brandon. He was suddenly aware of his disheveled appearance and felt self-conscious. It was too late to do anything about it now, except brush his hair back. A moment later they were standing right in front of him.

Doug grabbed Brandon's hand and shook it, at the same time saying, "Brandon, I want you to meet Andrea Granger. Andrea, this is Brandon Shaw, the man I have told you about for so long…so long."

"Glad to meet you, Mr. Shaw," Andrea said, extending her hand. "You are something of a legend in Florida."

Andrea was wearing a tan colored spring outfit with a skirt cut at mid-calf. The blouse was collared and buttoned down the front. She wore clips in her hair, which fell almost to the middle of her back. She was drop dead beautiful. Brandon Shaw felt his stomach go tight. This woman was trouble if ever he saw trouble, starting with his reaction to her, which was far stronger than he was comfortable with. Topping it all were blue eyes that pierced right into his soul. *Shit!* he thought. *What's going on?*

For a moment, Brandon just stood there, dumbfounded. Andrea's impeccable presence made him painfully aware of his own appearance, attired in a rumpled khaki safari shirt and matching shorts. He was normally clean shaven, but not today, his hangover had prevented any normal toilette when he finally struggled out of bed to make this trip to the airport. But goddammit, he would have shaved if he had known *she* was going to be here. Damn Doug anyway!

Brandon Shaw was six foot two inches tall, but at the moment, he felt smaller. What was supposed to come next?

Doug came to the rescue by saying, "Uh, it's been a long trip from Gainsville... Long trip. How 'bout we go get some lunch?"

"I'll vote for that," Brandon said, sounding clumsy, more like a schoolboy than the jungle icon of repute. The trio turned and walked through the terminal, exiting through one of the side doors which led to the plane. Brandon advised Lorenzo of their plans, asked him to baby sit the plane and promised to bring something back for him to eat. Actually, it was a little early for lunch, but right now Brandon wanted anything for a distraction. He needed to get a grip on this feeling in his stomach, an apprehension which he did not understand at all.

Several taxis waited in queue in front of the terminal. The trio grabbed one.

Brandon said, "Las Palmas," and they were on their way.

The Las Palmas restaurant was appropriately named. The interior was festooned with several large terra cotta pots hosting an assortment of palms. The roof of the place had enough skylights to support the light needs of the plants. The overall effect was very tropical and relaxing. It justified the slightly high prices and uniformed waiters.

When the trio had settled at a table, a waiter approached

and greeted them, then asked for their drink orders. Andrea said, "You know, it's kind of early, but I think I'd like to have something tropical with a little rum in it."

Brandon was next. "Yeah, me too," he said to the waiter with a wry smile. "Let me have something tropical with rum in it. Like for instance, a glass with some ice and rum." He looked at Andrea. "I just love ice."

Doug declined. "I'm flying." And vied for a lemonade.

The drinks had not arrived before Brandon turned to Andrea and stared at her hard. "Why are you here?" he asked.

Andrea appeared slightly taken aback by his directness but recovered. "Well," she explained. "I've been working at the compound in Gainsville for about six months now. It's always fascinated me to see Doug returning from down here, and the things he brings. It's kind of like Christmas, uncrating all the new animals."

"Christmas," Brandon said, absently.

The drinks arrived. Brandon took a deep sip. "So, you're here out of curiosity?" He smiled a knowing smile at Andrea.

"Well," Andrea hesitated a brief moment, "I'm also here to learn."

"Learn?" Brandon repeated. "Learn what?"

"All that you'll teach me," she replied. Then she looked at Doug for help.

"I'm guessing," Doug said, "Judging from your reaction, that you didn't get my email…uh, my email."

"Email?" Brandon repeated. "What email?"

"I sent you a long email three days ago, telling you about Andrea, about Andrea, the fact that she was coming down here to stay with you for a while."

"What?" Brandon said in mild alarm. "What do you mean, 'stay with me'?"

Doug continued. "Andrea has been working for us about six months now. It's amazing how much she's learned. Amazing.

She's also read everything there is to read about you. She wants to come down here and study under your tutelage…study."

"Under my what? Did anybody think of asking me about this?"

"Yes," Doug replied. "That's what the email was about."

"Oh, goddamn some frapping email!" Brandon spat. "You know I hate computers. I don't look at that thing more than once or twice a month."

"Well, maybe you should look at it more often," Doug attempted to sound offended.

"Why? So, I can learn how to Google, or Tweet, and whatever the hell else people do with those things. The day Brandon Shaw starts 'tweeting' is the day I start to shit bird seed."

"Okay, okay. Just calm down a little, a little." Doug tried to say in a soothing voice.

"No. Calming down doesn't seem to be on the menu here." Brandon forced himself to look at the menu just handed him. "My suggestion is, Ms. Granger, that we all have a nice relaxing lunch. You get about half in the bag, then climb back on that airplane and enjoy your ride back to Florida. With luck, you can be back in Gainsville by dark."

Now it was Andrea's turn to be direct. "What are you afraid of, Mr. Shaw?"

"Afraid? I'm not afraid of a damn thing. I just don't need a woman to baby sit at Jungle Cargo. Besides, we don't have any spare rooms in that little house. There's no place for you to bunk."

"That's bullshit, and you know it," Doug said. "That's a three-bedroom house."

"Yeah, and I have two of those bedrooms filled with boxes and all sorts of crap."

"So? Move the crap out of one of the rooms and make space for a guest. We're only talking about a couple of weeks."

"Two weeks," Brandon said, rolling his eyes. "Fish and house guests begin to stink after three days."

"I wouldn't be your house guest," Andrea said. "I would be your protégé. I expect to work and pull my weight while I'm at Jungle Cargo."

"I need a protégé about like I need an extra set of nuts," Brandon snapped. "We have no room for you at Jungle Cargo. Not only that, the lifestyle out there doesn't befit anyone that looks like you."

"What lifestyle could that possibly be?" Andrea asked.

"What lifestyle? Well, there's a lot of drinking and whoring that goes on out there. People walking around mostly naked. Frequently, old floozies walking around completely naked! We get drunk and piss on the trees... I don't want to have to explain all this to you. I'm sorry, but request denied."

Andrea tried to suppress a laugh when hearing the word, 'floozies'. "I'm sorry you feel that way."

"It's for the best," Brandon concluded. "Believe me, you would not be comfortable out there."

"I didn't come down here to be comfortable," Andrea said, with determination. "I came down here to work and learn."

"Learn what?" Brandon demanded. "There's nothing to learn. Well, wait a minute. I take that back. You could learn just how many new laws there are being enacted to protect wildlife. They don't make a damn difference on this end because we can pay people off. But U.S. Customs doesn't have any sense of humor. They'd seize the animals and file charges against us. So, what you can learn is that Jungle Cargo is on the hairy edge of being legislated out of business. Don't look now, but this is a business on the brink of extinction.

"What else? You could learn that I live like a fricking caveman. I drink way too much, I consort with other drunks and whores. My life is at a dead end. Legend? Legend of what? Legend, my ass. Our company is at the end of the road. You say you've been working with us for six months. Haven't you figured that out by now?"

"Yes, I have," Andrea said defensively. "But you know what? I've also figured out more. There might be some options available to you that you've never considered which could keep Jungle Cargo alive and well."

"You're a dreamer," Brandon quipped.

"Maybe. But wouldn't it be worth letting me hang around for a few weeks to find out? Even if there was nothing more than a slim chance for survival, that would be better than no chance. Maybe there are things we can learn from each other."

Brandon sat quietly for a long moment. He stared across the table at Andrea like a cat sizing up a mouse. He then decided to change the subject. "How are things in Gainsville?"

That question seemed to unleash a disquieting topic for Doug Bennet. "Not good," he said, as if somebody just let the air out of him. "Gainsville has been an old school college town for decades...decades. Now, something is going terribly wrong. It's turning into a swamp...a swamp." He shook his head vigorously back and forth.

"What are you talking about?" Brandon asked.

"Gangs are sprouting up. Crime is on the rise. Drugs. There are drugs coming in somehow. My God, we've never had a drug problem before in Gainsville. Never... never. You know Cali Spencer?"

"Yeah?" Brandon said, tensing up.

"Well...well, Cali's dead. Overdosed on drugs, heroin they say...heroin."

When Doug said that, Brandon looked as if he had just been stung by a scorpion. He started to say something when suddenly, Julio, the youngster from Sambala, came rushing into the restaurant, and straight to their table.

"Don Brandon," he gasped, out of breath. "You must

come to Sambala immediately. Naja is loose inside that temple. She may have killed a child."

"Good God!" Brandon said.

The trio rose and rushed outside to hail a taxi. Brandon grabbed the seat beside the driver. Andrea and Doug quickly piled in the back seat.

"Sambala, rapido!" Brandon demanded.

CHAPTER THREE

Naja Comes Home

IF THE RIDE INTO TOWN IN THE TRUCK SEEMED MISERABLE, THE return trip to Cuyamel and beyond, to the village of Sambala was downright torture. As skilled as the taxi driver was, it was impossible for him to miss all the potholes in this road, essentially a bulldozed trail through the jungle.

The only thing all three passengers could do was to hang on for dear life, because this taxi driver was determined to deliver the great Brandon Shaw to his appointment with destiny in as little time as possible.

After what seemed like forever, they turned left, off the main road, onto a narrower dirt road which led down the hill to Sambala. No instructions were needed. He knew exactly where to find the Temple of The Black Jaguar. Using his horn to clear the way of pedestrians in this small, narrow street village, he came to a skidding stop in front of the temple, a cloud of dust following close behind like a shadow.

Everybody disembarked. Brandon and Doug strode up the temple steps. Smoke Jaguar hadn't moved for hours. He stood, leaning back against the double entrance doors of the temple, still clutching the straw basket of Limpiras, tight against his chest. Brandon glared hard at the charlatan priest. And then Smoke Jaguar made his biggest mistake to date. He started speaking. "What you doin' here? You not needed here."

Brandon said one word. "Move!"

Smoke Jaguar became defiant, which was his next big mistake. "I no have to move. This my temple, my jaguar, my problem."

Upon hearing that, Brandon struck almost quicker than the eye could see, striking Smoke Jaguar across the side of the face and sending him tumbling down the steps. The priest lost his grip on the straw basket and paper money flew in every direction.

Smoke Jaguar finally stopped rolling about ten feet from the bottom of the steps, clearly unconscious.

Brandon turned to Doug as he opened one of the doors wide enough to slip through. "Close this door behind me and have somebody go to the local trucha and get me some rope, about ten feet of it."

Doug nodded. A villager had overheard the conversation and dashed away to retrieve the rope.

Inside the temple, darkness greeted Brandon Shaw. Whatever had provided illumination during Smoke Jaguar's rant had long since depleted its fuel and left nothing but the slight odor of kerosene. And somewhere in the darkness, a pissed off jaguar hid and waited for Brandon to make the wrong move.

What the hell was he doing here? He pondered, feeling for a pew to sit in long enough for his eyes to become adjusted to the dark. And how in the bleeding hell did he ever let himself get blackmailed into letting this insane voodoo priest have possession of Naja even for a moment. It was a regret he would take to his grave.

He remembered finding her in the jungle near Copan, mewing at the side of her dead mother. He had brought her home and raised her like she was a child more than a jungle beast. And she had reciprocated by loving him. Then he had done this to her. Wherever she was in this room, she was probably thinking about the same thing, that the one person in the world she had ever trusted had turned his back on her and placed her into the hands of a maniac. Damn it all anyway.

Brandon called on one of his exceptional senses to make a determination. He smelled no blood. That was good news. But his eyes were having trouble adjusting to the dark after being exposed to the brightness outside for so long. He felt his way along the center aisle by touching the back of each pew as he made his way forward to the dais. By the time he reached the platform, he could hear the soft sounds of whimpering coming from his left.

He turned and worked his way toward the sound and found Evaristo against the wall, sitting on the floor, in shock but otherwise unharmed. He knew damn well Naja would never hurt a child. She loved playing with children.

He spoke gently to the boy, saying, "Come with me. Put your arms around my neck. Everything is going to be all right."

Evaristo complied. He gladly grabbed Brandon around the neck and Brandon made his way back to the front doors.

During this short journey, Brandon heard the sound of distant thunder. Thunderstorms could make their way down off the sides of the mountains a kilometer back from the coast, very quickly this time of year.

Slowly, Brandon made his way to the double doors and half whispered to Doug to open them. Doug untied the rope and eased one door open. Brandon handed Evaristo to Andrea.

Evaristo's mother stood behind them at the base of the temple steps. When she saw her baby, she started sobbing and rushed up the steps to take him from Andrea. "Oh, gracias a Dios. Gracias Don Brandon! Mi hijo!" She retreated down the steps with her child, and then down the street, toward her house to properly tend to him.

Meanwhile, Brandon glanced at the ominous, darkening skies. Then he slowly pulled the door closed again and returned to his task.

Somewhere in the darkness the black jaguar waited, frightened, furious and on the defensive from endless abuse he guessed. And now, Brandon Shaw was all alone with her.

"Naja," he said as softly and soothingly as he knew how. The response was a long, low growl that reverberated throughout the room and was hard to pinpoint. "Naja, it's me!"

Surely, she could smell him and identify his familiar scent, but for one hitch. He had been drinking so heavily lately that he reeked of alcohol. If she couldn't recognize his odor, he was in big trouble.

Naja's refusal to respond positively to Brandon's voice was more than upsetting. It was a warning, and he realized he'd been cloaking the truth from himself. Naja knew who was there. She knew and was no doubt furious with him.

He tried calling her again, this time with more of a master's voice. His entreaty was answered with a warning growl.

Thunder peeled, this time much closer and louder. "Great!" Brandon thought. Naja wasn't upset enough, now the skies were plotting against him.

Finally, in exasperation and because he knew he was running out of time before the rain started and made its own thunder on this tin roof, Brandon called to her one more time. This time, with authority. "Naja, come here to me!" With that, there was one more growl, only this one was different. It said, "Here I come!"

Naja, who could see perfectly in the darkness, launched herself through the air, colliding with Brandon broadside with all her 300 pounds. The impact of the terrible crash propelled them both sideways, into the pews.

Brandon lay on his back on the floor with Naja on top of him. This is normally a kill position for a jungle cat because they use the claws on their back feet to disembowel their prey. For some reason known only to Naja, she did not do that. Brandon gripped her by the throat and kept her at arm's length while yelling, "Goddammit, Naja! It's me. It's me!"

Somehow, he managed to get out from under her and reverse positions, with her on the bottom. But she was too much for Brandon. He lost his grip and Naja rose, grabbing him on the inner thigh with her powerful mouth and biting down hard. Brandon's pain caused a long agonizing scream.

Meanwhile, Doug and Andrea listened intently to the ruckus from outside. What they heard sent chills up Andrea's spine. She heard Brandon order Naja to him; and then she heard the terrible crash as they fell into the pews, scattering them in the fight that ensued. She heard Naja's roar. She heard Brandon cursing. She heard the approaching thunder. Then, when Naja managed to bite Brandon, she heard a blood curdling scream of pain, but also something else. It took a moment or two for her to realize what she was hearing, but when she did, her eyes widened, and goose bumps formed on her arms.

One moment, Brandon was screaming. In that same moment, she heard Naja growling. But then, his screams stopped. Instead, she distinctly heard two separate jaguar roars. It could not have been her imagination. She looked at Doug and stammered, "What the hell?"

Doug looked at her, slightly confused. "I don't know, don't know. What are you talking about?"

Andrea narrowed her eyes. "You know damn well what I'm talking about. I just heard TWO jaguars roaring inside there, not one, but two. Is there a second cat in there that we didn't know about?"

Doug shook his head. "No. I think you're hearing things. Hearing things."

Now Andrea was mad. "Bullshit! Like hell I am. My hearing is not that bad, and I haven't been drinking. I know what I heard."

At that very moment, she heard Brandon's voice from just inside the doors. "Has that rope gotten here yet?"

Julio, who had managed to arrive, ran up the steps and handed a length of rope to Doug, who cracked the door slightly and passed it through to Brandon. A few moments later, Brandon said, "Okay, you can open the doors now. Everything is under control."

Doug complied and swung the doors open wide. There stood Brandon, Naja at his side, as calm as a kitten, panting slightly, with a little bit of Brandon's blood around her mouth, but otherwise appearing harmless and tame.

Brandon on the other hand was bleeding profusely from his left inner thigh and looked as pale as mashed potatoes. Clearly, without immediate medical attention, he would bleed out. Doug ripped off his own belt and wrapped it around Brandon's upper leg, making it into a tourniquet. Brandon began to sag. Thunder rolled and drops of rain started to stain the dry concrete of the temple steps and landing. Brandon looked up, smiled at the thunder and uttered, "Chak speaks!"

Andrea did not understand. "Who's Chak?" she asked. But there was no time for an answer. Brandon fell forward. Doug did his best to catch him.

Brandon's last words before passing out were, "Take Naja home. She's been through enough." His words were slurred and hard to understand. But Julio bravely took the rope leash and headed for the beach and the one kilometer trek to Jungle Cargo, Naja walking happily by his side like a family dog.

CHAPTER FOUR

"Home to Jungle Cargo aka / The Reception"

"He's down, deep inside somewhere, healing himself. This isn't his first time at the rodeo, for sure. I've patched him up several times. The good news is the man has an incredible recovery ability."

Andrea and Doug stood on one side of Brandon's bed in the Mazapan Hospital ER section. Dr. Humberto Dominguez stood on the opposite side, speaking softly about his patient.

Dr. Humberto Dominguez (Doc) was a slender, balding Honduran in his 50s who spoke surprisingly good English. Dark skinned, clean shaven, he looked deceptively doctor-like in his white smock. He was also a long-time friend of Brandon Shaw and had attended him more than once following one mishap or another.

But most of all, Doc was a party goer and there was nothing in the world he liked better than to drink the day away while the barbeque pit slowly cooked one kind of meat or another. He didn't really care what was cooking, but Jungle Cargo was where he liked to eat it. So, most weekends were spent as a house guest at Cuyamel. This was necessary because when Doc wound down from partying, he was certainly in no shape to drive anywhere, much less negotiate that obstacle course of a road back to town.

Andrea held the side rail on the hospital bed very firmly and looked down, into the face of Brandon Shaw, still sleeping following surgery.

She did not like what she saw; for what she saw was destiny. Her destiny, and it disturbed her greatly.

"Let's get out of here," she said to no one in particular. She then seemed to pull back to the present and glanced at Doug and Dr. Dominguez.

"There's nothing we can do for a while. Nurse Rosa is there," she nodded, indicating the nurse sitting in a chair a few feet from the bed, "she's here to take care of him." Her sentence seemed unfinished, but she stopped talking.

Dr. Dominguez checked his wristwatch.

"Well, I've got rounds to make. I'd like to join you two." The doctor smiled and shook his head. "Maybe later."

The trio left the room. In the hallway, Dr. Dominguez shook hands with Andrea and Doug, then made his apologies and walked down the hall.

Andrea watched him go, then said, "Let's get out of here. There's something I need to talk about."

"Want to go to the cafeteria?" Doug asked.

Andrea shook her head. "No, everything in that place tastes pre-digested. I want to get out of this hospital for a while." She headed for the front door.

The Mazapan Hospital was located in downtown LaCeiba and not separated from the rest of society the way hospitals are in the U.S. Once outside, Andrea and Doug found themselves on a busy city sidewalk. They walked a couple of blocks to where a sidewalk café sprawled out with tables and large umbrellas. It looked inviting, so they seated themselves. After ordering coffee and fresh fruit, Andrea began to calm down a little, but something was clearly on her mind.

Doug eyed her, but remained silent, waiting for her to open up. He wasn't sure what to expect.

Finally, she said, "I want to talk about what happened at that damned temple, or whatever that perversion is."

"Okay," Doug said, sipping his coffee. "What's bothering you? Uh, bothering you?"

Andrea squeezed lime juice onto a piece of cantaloupe before cutting a bite sized chunk. "You know what's on my mind as well as I do." Andrea looked at Doug accusingly. "When Brandon was in that… 'temple,' something other worldly happened. Don't deny it. I saw the look on your face. I want to know what you know."

Doug looked Andrea in the eye. "Andrea, I don't know what you think you heard, what you heard. And I don't know anything more than you know."

Andrea peered at Doug sharply as she swallowed her cantaloupe. "My God, you're lying through your teeth! I thought we had a good relationship, Doug. One based on mutual respect and trust. I have never seen this side of you before. You do know what's going on and I'll guarantee you, before this is over, I will too."

Andrea spent the remainder of the meal fuming while Doug shrank from her fury.

When Doug and Andrea again arrived at the hospital room, they were greeted with a surprise. Brandon Shaw had regained consciousness and was rebelling at being in the hospital. Doc Dominguez was trying to calm him.

"I've got an animal compound to run. I don't have time to lay around here like some pussy."

"Things at the compound are fine. They are under control," Doc said.

"How?" Brandon demanded. "How can things be so under control when I'm not there?"

"Because someone is running it for you."

Brandon pulled up short. "What? Who?"

"I am," Andrea said, stepping forward, arms crossed, ready for anything that happened.

"Yes," Doug chimed in, hoping to head off a donnybrook. "And she's doing a damn fine job of it, damn fine job. And now that I see you are with us again, I can quit worrying and get that plane back to Gainsville. I've got a compound there to run too, you know. Plus, the animals on board are stressing very badly by now. So, so, I'm gone. Goodbye!"

With no other formality, more like he was escaping from an ugly situation, Doug turned and disappeared down the hall without further commentary.

Brandon, preoccupied with staring at Andrea, didn't notice that Doug had departed.

Andrea stared back until she became tired of the game. Finally, she said, "You have something you want to say?"

Brandon thought about it for a minute, now staring at the end of his bed. "I guess I need to say thank you," he stammered. "How long have I been out of it anyway?"

"Three days," Andrea said as she took a seat next to his bed. "Naja mauled you, severed an artery. You lost a lot of blood. It's a wonder we didn't lose you. Luckily, we got a military chopper to come to Sambala and life-flight you here, to the hospital. I'm sure that factor alone saved you. Then it was your good fortune that the hospital had blood in stock that matched your type. All in all, the winds of fortune were in your favor, Bwana. Otherwise, we'd all be attending your funeral right about now."

Brandon felt humbled, and it showed on his face, in his eyes. "It was that bad, huh?"

"It *was* that bad," Andrea repeated. "Lucky for you, you

seem to have a lot of very devoted people around you, as well as good friends. Everyone at Jungle Cargo is very concerned. The girls have spent as much time praying for you as they have working."

Brandon smiled, then thought about something. "Where is Naja?"

"Naja is fine. She's safe in her run at the compound. She was a little emaciated, dehydrated; so, Lorenzo is giving her lots of TLC as well as a lot of groceries. I can see an improvement already.

"What I don't understand is what she was doing in the possession of that lunatic in Sambala in the first place." She looked at Brandon quizzically.

Brandon shook his head, thinking about the horrible breach that placed Naja in possession of the cultist priest. "It's a long and very perverted story. Maybe when I feel better, but please, not now."

"Fair enough," Andrea said, and dismissed the subject.

Although he had only been awake for a brief time, Andrea could see that Brandon was becoming groggy. He closed his eyes and leaned to one side. Both Andrea and the attending nurse rose to catch him and lay him back in bed. It was just as well. Brandon needed to heal, and Andrea needed to return to Jungle Cargo and take care of the business of running an animal compound.

When she drove the company jeep into town the next day to visit Brandon, she never expected to witness the scene which played out in Brandon's hospital room. Even before she got to the room, she could hear the loud, uncultured female voice issuing from inside the ICU room. "Oui, my love. Pobrecito. Let me fix your pillow un poquito."

Andrea stepped inside the doorway of the room to see an overweight, buxom Hispanic woman in her 40s, wearing far too much makeup which included bright red lipstick that she managed to smear all over Brandon's face.

The woman wore a brown tight skirt which seemed a couple of sizes too small for her, but it helped to complete the image of someone Brandon had probably been referring to when he spoke of the 'floozies' that frequented Jungle Cargo.

Brandon was obviously perturbed and more than a little embarrassed at the woman's display. Marta Saldana, a "something to do on Saturday night" acquaintance of Brandon's who had suddenly become very possessive when she heard of the blonde woman from the United States, here to invade her territory, albeit it highly unlikely there was any territory to invade.

When Marta Saldana realized Andrea had entered the room, she looked up at her with darts in her eyes, then opted to ignore her and continued with her over-the-top affectionate attentions to the consternated Brandon Shaw.

"Aye, Corazon. You know I'm going to take very good care of you. I would have been here sooner, but nobody told me anything. I had to read about it in La Prensa."

Andrea couldn't hide her amusement and therefore left the room and Brandon Shaw to his dilemma. She walked toward the cafeteria, leaving the sounds of Marta Saldana and her histrionic cooing behind.

In the cafeteria, she found a newspaper lying on one counter where she found the front-page story of Brandon Shaw rescuing Evaristo from the deadly, marauding jungle cat, blah blah. The reporters for La Prensa were only a few days late, but that was nothing unusual in Honduras, where just about everything moved slowly.

———

Three scant days later, Doc Dominguez was more than ready

to discharge Don Brandon. It was more like evict him. "It's time to get my old friend out of here before he turns this hospital upside down," Doc said as he and Andrea strode hurriedly down the corridor side by side.

"What's going on?" Andrea asked.

"Brandon...is what's going on. Typical Brandon Shaw. It would be simpler to keep Naja penned up. He's cranky, curses everything and everybody. He threw a tray of food up against the wall yesterday. Said it smelled like...well, you know. He's got all the nurses intimidated. Well...all except for one. He has her in a different kind of dither. We caught her in the act of, uh, satisfying one of his needs at two o'clock this morning. And, we couldn't fire her. She is the head nurse on the shift." Then Doc paused and realized what he had said, started chuckling softly. "Well, maybe *head nurse* is the proper term for her." Then he really started laughing. Andrea just looked at the ceiling.

As they walked into Brandon's room, Doc stopped laughing and addressed his patient. "I'm kicking you out of here, you sonofabitch, before you wreck the whole hospital."

"Good!" Brandon said. "The sooner the better."

"Well, it's going to be sooner. I don't know if Andrea has room for you in the jeep or not, but I'm driving you to Cuyamel in my car. That way, I'll make sure those stitches stay put and you don't have an excuse to come back here."

"You're a gem!" Brandon said, half smiling. His left leg was heavily bandaged, and he had been provided with crutches. Two nurses came into the room to help get him dressed. Andrea gathered his other things.

A wheel-chair was brought in and Brandon Shaw was unceremoniously moved from the bed to the wheelchair, then escorted down the hall to the patient's exit.

But it became evident the moment everybody left the hospital that being a passenger in Doc's car would be a near impossibility. His small car was loaded, including the trunk and all seats save the driver's seat with party supplies.

"Oh!" he said. "I forgot completely about this stuff. I guess you'll have to ride with Andrea after all!"

Brandon looked at Doc with one squinted eye.

Andrea shook her head and went to get the Jeep.

The ride from LaCeiba to Cuyamel was slower and more trepidatious than usual. Missing the potholes was one thing but swerves to do so had to be adroit and gentle. Be that as it may, there were still occasional grimaces when a sharper than desired veer became necessary.

Eventually, the two-vehicle convoy turned left off the highway onto the narrow, secondary road leading down to the beach and to Jungle Cargo.

Brandon began to perk up at this point, anticipating being home.

And then, they arrived, driving through the arched sign that announced they were at Jungle Cargo, at last.

As they entered Jungle Cargo proper through the archway, a warm and exciting scene greeted Brandon Shaw. The two Honduran girls, Anna Maria and Suyapa came running down the stairs from the house, squealing with excitement. The compound manager, Pablo Palma, looked up from his work and when he saw the convoy approaching, stopped what he was doing to walk over and greet his arriving boss.

Lorenzo appeared from the opposite side of the beach house with a huge smile. When the two vehicles came to a stop in front of the house,

Brandon's employees surrounded the Jeep. As Brandon tried to get out of the Jeep and onto his crutches, he required help from Pablo and Lorenzo.

Once accomplished, the small group headed for the breezeway beneath the house, where the two men had set up tables and chairs. Chatter and laughter filled the air as everybody helped Brandon get seated. Then beers appeared, with a bowl of key limes cut into quarters, plus a dish of salt. The welcome home party had officially started.

But one *party* didn't like being left out one bit. Naja, upon seeing Brandon, began pacing back and forth in her run making a pitiful mewing sound, looking toward her master non-stop. When no one seemed to notice her mewing, Naja roared a coughing roar which said, "What about me?" Brandon looked past everyone at the cat in her run in the compound. "Poor girl!" he said. After watching her pacing plea for a few more moments, he nodded at Pablo, "Go let her out, but bring her here on a leash."

Lorenzo looked slightly alarmed. He quickly said, "That's not a good idea, Jefe."

"And why not?" Brandon countered. "Look at her. She's going nuts wanting out of that damned cage. She wants to see me, to be with me."

"Yes, I know, but…," Lorenzo said.

It was too late. Pablo Palma stood ready at the door of the run with a leash in one hand. But when he opened the gate, Naja took off like lightning, knocking Pablo aside like a toy. She came at a full gallop toward Brandon. Everyone saw what was about to happen and took cover; all except for Brandon who could not move.

Like a puppy, except this puppy weighed 300 pounds, Naja launched herself into the air, flew over the table and landed squarely in Brandon's lap. The impact sent him reeling backwards several feet and onto the concrete slab. The table and its contents scattered. Chairs were overturned, beers, limes and salt hit the concrete floor.

Brandon lay flat on his back while Naja, above him, licked his face and lowered herself onto him to give him a jaguar hug. There were screams, cursing, and then laughter as everyone recovered. Most of all, Brandon laughed uncontrollably, despite the obvious pain he suffered. The scene, chaotic as it was, was the comic relief everyone needed. Doc had managed to reach Brandon's side and carefully inspected his stitches, all the while pushing an affectionate jaguar out of the way to do so. "Lucky." he managed to say. "Pinche' lucky."

It looked as though the remainder of the afternoon would pass with relative normality. Doc was being his typical cut-up self; joking, drinking, entertaining. Pablo was over-seeing the barbeque which cooked slowly, smoke curling lazily upward into the afternoon sky.

Late in the afternoon, the party got interrupted. First, the gathering in the carport heard jungle drums from not too far away. Then, a group of about forty or fifty villagers from Sambala appeared on the dirt path leading to the main road. They were adorned in strange costumes, many of which suggested strongly their African roots.

Sambala is one of the last surviving coastal villages that is a remnant of African origin. Most of the residents there are of African descent, even to the point of speaking Garifuna, a derivative of Swahili and other African based languages, as opposed to Spanish. Also, many of the customs and beliefs are of African origin, a factor which Smoke Jaguar had preyed upon.

Brandon struggled to his feet and, walking with the crutches, made his way to the dirt drive behind the house to see what was going on.

One rather tall young black man separated himself from the group and came toward Brandon, stopping a few feet in front of him. He was adorned in a bright costume made of brightly painted and decorated leather, which looked celebratory in nature, and his face and body were painted with white and red markings.

He addressed Brandon in a loud voice, then pointed at him

as he spoke in a language mixed with Garifuna and broken Spanish.

"Lord Brandon, we come here to honor you for saving our village from the black tigre and other evils imposed by the voodoo priest. You are Bwana to us, and we are grateful."

With that, the young villager backed away to rejoin the other performers and the pulsating drums, yet unseen, thundered to life and loudly began to beat a hypnotic rhythm. Andrea, Doc, Lorenzo, Pablo and the girls joined Brandon in watching this orchestrated performance.

First, a dancer came forward wearing a head-dress that represented Smoke Jaguar, as the depiction had an evil, uncomplimentary appearance. This dancer gyrated, raising his arms high and wide apart and positioning his hands like claws. Then, behind him appeared a second dancer who portrayed a pseudo Naja and this dancer had to mimic, clearly against the dancer's will, the movements of pseudo Smoke Jaguar.

Each chapter of the events which took place on that fateful Saturday were carefully choreographed to mimic the actions of the actual persons involved, and the one animal involved. It was surprisingly telling and artistic, and yet, somehow poignant; respectful in its telling of what had clearly become a folk tale to the villagers.

The dance reached a crescendo when suddenly, a second jaguar appeared out of nowhere and faced the first pseudo cat. These two circled each other for a moment as the dancers raised their arms up high. Then the second pseudo jaguar embraced pseudo Brandon and shucked his mask, circling around pseudo Brandon, but remaining close. The dance then ended with pseudo Brandon being carried away, wounded but triumphant.

After the performance ended, the performers withdrew and faded into the jungle undergrowth as quickly and quietly as they had appeared. The drums fell silent and the villagers were gone, as if they had been nothing more than an illusion.

Brandon stood motionless, balanced on his crutches, for several moments after the villagers evaporated back into the jungle. He froze in place, looking in the direction they had gone. He seemed in shock.

Finally, Andrea moved to his side, gently took his arm and said softly, "Well, it seems you are revered by the people of Sambala, 'Bwana'."

It took Brandon a moment to shake loose from his trance. Then, "Wow! What the hell was that all about?"

Doc, standing a few feet away said, "Well, I wasn't in Sambala, but unless I miss my guess, we just saw an interpretation of their take on the events the day you got fucked up. Excuse me, I mean mauled. I'd say they did a damn fine job of it."

Everyone turned and walked back toward the carport. Andrea stayed close to Brandon and took his arm, presumably to help steady him.

In the carport, she took a chair next to him and watched him closely while everyone drank and chatted the afternoon away. Brandon remained quiet, looking far away. Naja also stayed close at his side, lying on the concrete floor to get as cool as possible, panting lightly and looking out at the water which seemed closer than usual today.

Finally, Andrea broached a topic that bugged her. "That was quite a performance those villagers put together, huh? Choreographed and everything. Must have put a lot of effort into it, to say nothing of rehearsal?"

Brandon nodded agreement. "Yes, it was."

Andrea watched Brandon closely for his reaction to her next sentence. "I wonder what that interpretation of a second jaguar was all about? You know, the one that shadowed the Brandon dancer?"

Brandon looked straight at Andrea. "I don't know. They're villagers. They live by folk tales and all folk tales by nature are part bullshit. You know that."

The way he said it left no doubt that the subject was to be dropped. Andrea took a sip of her beer while still locking eyes with Brandon.

The next several days passed with relative normalcy considering this was the life of Brandon Shaw. Brandon languished, for the most part, allowing his body to heal. There were however the morning meetings, always held on the front deck of the house.

Every morning, the girls would prepare a table filled with bowls of fresh fruit and one bowl of hard-boiled eggs.

Pablo and Lorenzo would gather along with Andrea, Brandon and the girls to get their ducks in a row, discuss any problems, events or other business. One morning, Suyapa appeared with a small, baby monkey that seemed weak. "It just won't eat," she complained.

She gave the monkey to Brandon who stroked it and spoke to it softly. Within minutes the little animal reached up with its tiny hand to touch Brandon's face. Then it began taking pieces of banana and mango from Brandon's fingers and eating ravenously. Andrea watched this in amazement. This man possessed a special magic, she decided. There was no doubt about it. Brandon had a unique way that he communicated with animals, and they trusted him, even though they were wild children of the forest.

Andrea said nothing, but she now viewed Brandon Shaw with a different eye, with awe of his powers of recovery. Each week, Doc would carefully remove the dressing on Brandon's thigh for an inspection. And each week, the wound looked remarkably more healed, almost as if it had been something that happened long ago. Andrea remarked about this to Doc.

He nodded in agreement, saying, "I know. I've never seen

anything like it. Our friend and lord of the jungle has gotten banged up before. I used to worry until I finally figured out that he has exceptional recovery abilities."

"Exceptional?" Andrea countered.

"*Very* exceptional." Doc replied.

CHAPTER FIVE

Near Miss

THE RAINY SEASON PROGRESSED, AND AS IT DID SO, EVERY afternoon saw dark clouds work their way down from the mountains behind Jungle Cargo toward the sea, bringing with them a temporary respite from the oppressive heat. Such afternoons normally found Brandon napping in a chaise lounge on the deck, under the overhang of the roof where he could stay dry, but still be facing the blue Caribbean only yards away.

Andrea loved the rolling thunder in the jungle. She called it, "Stereo thunder." It would begin up high on the mountainside, then travel down the mountain, over the top of the house and out to sea. In her opinion, there was nothing quite like sipping a glass of ice-cold tea with lots of key lime juice and mint and listening to the thunder and the raindrops pattering on the jungle canopy. There was also the smell. The rain caused several varieties of jungle orchids to open and release their perfume. The air was filled with a very light, sweet aroma.

Such was this day. The girls had gone home early to Sambala

and the men were off doing something that kept them out of the rain. Andrea went to the kitchen to make her tea when she saw some movement outside, through the window. She just got a glance of whatever it was, but it looked out of place. She looked closer, but it wasn't there, so she cat walked through the house to the bedroom and peeked out the window there. Nothing. She carefully adjusted the shutters, so she could see more directly down. There it was. A human figure pressing hard against the side of the house and moving slowly, cautiously toward the front.

At this point, Andrea's instinct took over. She grabbed her Glock from her purse and made her way through the house swiftly, silently to the back steps. As stealthily as a cat, she descended the steps and crept around the corner of the house. By then, her target was making its way around the corner of the house to the front. As quickly as she could, Andrea caught up with this person and came up behind him. It was Smoke Jaguar, and he was armed with a very large 357 magnum revolver.

Smoke Jaguar was so riveted on his target that he was completely unaware of Andrea only inches behind him, pointing her gun at his head. Smoke Jaguar was after Brandon. He was peering up, through the spaces between the boards of the deck to make out the silhouette of his victim-to-be. And now he saw and identified what he was looking for, Brandon Shaw, asleep in the chaise lounge. He extended his arms up and aimed the 357 at Brandon.

It was at that moment that Andrea pushed her Glock hard against the back of Smoke Jaguar's head and said, "If you pull that trigger, it'll be the last thing you ever do on this earth. Put the gun down."

Smoke Jaguar, taken by surprise, froze. He could not believe that he had been caught in his plot for revenge. A moment later, Andrea repeated her command. "You have until the count of three. Then I'm going to blow your brains all over the beach. One… two…"

Smoke Jaguar dropped the gun. He turned slowly to look at Andrea, his eyes as big as silver dollars with fear. Andrea gave him her most fearsome glare as she said in a voice loud enough for Brandon to hear, "Brandon, you've got a visitor!"

Above their heads, she heard Brandon stirring. "What?" he said as he woke up.

Andrea never took her eyes, or her gun off the intruder. "Yeah. Smoke Jaguar, or whatever this asshole's real name is, decided to pay you a visit." Suddenly she heard her boss get up out of the chaise lounge and make his way across the deck to the staircase, then down the stairs. A moment later, Brandon limped toward Andrea and her captive.

"What the hell is going on here?" Brandon demanded.

Andrea continued to glare at Smoke Jaguar. "I caught this guy sneaking up on you. His apparent plan was to shoot you from down here, like the coward he is."

Brandon looked to the ground and saw Smoke Jaguar's 357 lying on the sand. He stooped quickly and picked it up. Instinctively, he opened the gun and checked to see if it was loaded. It was. He then closed the weapon. He looked at Smoke Jaguar with fire in his eyes. "Was that your plan? Huh? Say something, you bastard. What in the hell were you gonna do, assassinate me? Shoot me while I slept? Is that the kind of sneak piss ant you are? You chicken-shit son of a whore?"

Brandon exploded. Faster than the eye could see, he slugged the voodoo priest. There was a sickening sound of fist hitting against flesh so hard that something in that face, bone or cartilage must have broken.

Smoke Jaguar reeled. He hit the sand, half unconscious and should have stayed there; but numb and not thinking because of the impact, he made the mistake of trying to get up. It was a bad decision. Brandon was on him again and hit him with even more force than the first time. Smoke Jaguar reeled and staggered toward the beach. Brandon was right behind him. Balancing on his bandaged leg, Brandon managed to use his good leg to kick Smoke Jaguar squarely between the legs. Smoke Jaguar uttered a guttural cry of pain, staggered a couple of steps forward and fell to the sand like a bag of wet laundry. The sand around his face began to turn red from blood.

Brandon stood over the fallen man, reached down and turned him over on his back. After staring at him a moment, he cocked Smoke Jaguar's 357 and aimed it at his face. At this point, Andrea interrupted. "No Brandon, don't do it."

"Why not?" Brandon snarled as he looked into the face of Smoke Jaguar.

"Because, if you kill him, you'll wind up in a Honduran jail, probably forever. It's not worth it. Besides, if you kill him, his suffering will be over. There are ways to make him suffer worse by letting him live."

Brandon thought about Andrea's words for a long minute. He then aimed the gun ever so slightly to the right of Smoke Jaguar's head and pulled the trigger. There was a loud report. Smoke Jaguar screamed in pain and grabbed his left ear, even as a trickle of blood began to come from that side of his head.

"Maybe you have a point," Brandon said. He turned and made his way back to the house, up the stairs. Andrea was close at his heels. They both left Smoke Jaguar to his own devices, lying on the sand, bleeding and half unconscious, obviously in extreme pain.

When they were back up on the deck, Brandon retrieved a towel from the chaise lounge to wipe the rain from his face. He then handed the towel to Andrea. "You saved my life," he said. "I owe you."

Andrea shook her head. "You would have done the same for me."

At that moment, heavy footsteps were heard on the deck stairs. Seconds later, an alarmed Lorenzo Ponce and Pablo Palma appeared on the deck. Brandon looked at them. "Go get that piece of shit down there and drag him a hundred yards or so down the beach. I don't want him stinking the place up around here." Without a word, the two men retreated down the stairs to follow their boss's order. By now Naja was aware of Smoke Jaguar's presence and roared loudly in her run. As if joining her, thunder rolled across the sky and the rain began to fall harder.

Brandon regained his seat in the chaise lounge. Andrea pulled a deck chair up beside him and sat quietly, listening to the patter of the rain on the palm fronds and nearby jungle canopy. Rain also had the effect of flattening the waves in front of the house. Andrea compared it to God gently petting a giant beast.

As Brandon looked out at the water, he said, obviously to Andrea, "You handle a gun pretty well, for a woman."

"Quit being sexist," Andrea said with a half-smile. "I do a lot of things well, 'for a woman'."

"I wasn't aware that you were carrying a piece. You must have brought it from the States."

"Yes."

"So, how did you get it past customs? They have kind of a thing here about guns, especially pistolas that aren't used for dove hunting."

"I have a permit."

Brandon was quiet for several moments, then said,

"That must be some permit!"

Andrea said nothing. The rain was falling harder and that filled the silence. Brandon slowly dozed, leaving Andrea alone with her thoughts.

The next several days were uneventful at Jungle Cargo. Business was as usual, with Indians bringing animals in from the jungle to sell. Lorenzo and Andrea tried as much as possible not to bother Brandon with mundane details. But occasionally someone would arrive with a large snake in a box or bag and this was Brandon's area.

Most of the snakes were of the same species; the very large and extremely deadly fer-de-lance. The local Indians had several names for it, none of which were complimentary and in fact, one of them ominous. They called it 'yellow beard' because of the long yellow line along its lower jaw. Other names were, 'lance head' because of the pronounced triangular shape of its head, 'four noses' because the loreal pits in the pit viper's face looked like nostrils. And finally, they called it "Seis pie" or 'six steps' because that is how far a person could walk after being bitten by one before collapsing and dying. A slight exaggeration to be sure, but a dire warning none-the-less.

As macho as Lorenzo tried to think himself to be, he shrunk from the idea of estimating the size and worth of the vipers. The snake was large, powerful and possessed exceedingly long hypodermic fangs plus very large venom glands.

A bite from this reptile is a kiss goodbye unless the proper first aid is close at hand and lots of anti-venom. Lorenzo was happy to leave such decisions to his boss, Don Brandon Shaw, and Don Brandon had a precarious way of examining each snake coming into the compound. He wound dump it out of whatever container the hunter had brought it in and visually inspect each creature. He had done this for so many years that there was no need to seize it and stretch it out in the measuring box. Brandon could nail it every time to within a couple of inches, and since capturing such reptiles was dangerous, he was always generous and added at least a half foot onto the snake's actual length.

The hunters knew this and trusted him. There was never a dispute. Brandon would inspect the snake, pay the hunter who would thank him and retreat back into the jungle. Lorenzo would use large, long metal tongs to pick up the snake and take it to the in-ground pit, where it would be added to the other snakes.

Andrea would have wondered why Brandon needed so many snakes except that he had a standing order for them from some laboratory in Florida which she assumed was doing research with the venom. Odd though; when Doug would make a trip down here to bring a load of animals back to Florida, the customer, Dr. Felipe Quintanilla would always be waiting at the Miami airport to collect his shipment. He was always in such a hurry to receive the boxes and did not want them sent to him in Ocala. Plus, to Andrea's way of thinking, Dr. Quintanilla was not a very nice guy. In fact, he didn't seem much like a doctor at all. He was always so brusque, and in Andrea's opinion, coarse.

Instincts. They were important, Andrea mused, especially to a woman because being right often shifted circumstances dramatically. And her instincts about Dr. Quintanilla told her he was rotten to the core.

A day or so later, an Indian showed up, out of the jungle with a different kind of snake, one that Andrea thought she recognized as a jumping viper; but she didn't know what the price for it would be. Besides, once again, it was a snake, and this was Brandon's purview. But Brandon was nowhere to be found. Andrea looked around downstairs. She called up to Suyapa. "Hija, have you seen Don Brandon?"

Suyapa stopped her sweeping for a moment. "I think I saw him walking down the beach with Naja." She pointed west.

"Gracias," Andrea said, asked the Indian to wait while she looked for Brandon, then walked toward the beach, turning left. About two hundred yards down the beach, she spotted Brandon. He was sitting on a large boulder, and Naja was perched directly in front of him, looking up at him. It seemed like Brandon was speaking to the big cat, and she was thoroughly engrossed in what he was saying, a highly unlikely probability, and yet…

When Andrea approached within fifty yards or so, Naja noticed her and turned her head to look at her. That's when Brandon also turned to look her way and the conversation, or whatever, came to an abrupt halt.

"Hi there!" Andrea said, ignoring what she thought she had just seen.

"Hi," Brandon responded. "What's up?"

"Oh, I came to get you because there's an Indian waiting for you with a snake."

"Really? What kind?"

"I'm not sure," Andrea said. "I think it's a jumping viper. Has a nasty disposition. In any case, none of us knows how much to pay for it."

Brandon shook his head. "They aren't worth much. But I buy them just to keep the hunters from getting discouraged. What makes any animal, especially snakes valuable is a plentiful supply of one kind. The fer-de-lance for example. There's a reliable enough number of them that the laboratory can use their venom for research, and, or, drug production."

"I see," Andrea replied as Brandon got to his feet and they began to walk back toward the compound. They walked slowly, but Andrea noticed that Brandon was depending less on his cane each day. In fact, he was almost walking without a limp.

After a minute or so in silence, Brandon said, "I need to thank you for everything you've done since being here. I admit, I didn't want you here at first, but I never envisioned the way it would actually be."

Andrea smiled without looking up at him. "Oh, you're welcome. I've learned a lot since being here. Besides, I know how it is with bachelors."

"Well, the thing is, I'm not really a bachelor at heart. It just seems that my lifestyle doesn't mesh very well with relationships. Not long-term relationships anyway."

"Oh? And why not?" Andrea asked.

Brandon shook his head. "Dunno. I mean, I bathe regularly, and…"

"Drink too much," Andrea interjected.

"Yeah," Brandon agreed. "Probably so. But I didn't always."

"Why do you now?"

Brandon stopped walking, looked far away, at nothing in particular. "Don't know that either. Maybe this lifestyle is getting to me too."

Then he resumed his pace toward the house. There was no more talking along the way, just sort of an aura, a communion with nature. Andrea watched as a mob of yellow naped amazon parrots flew low overhead making a raucous noise. It was a reminder that here was one of the last bastions on earth of nature as it was and should be. It was a good feeling to be here.

Naja suddenly broke away and started chasing a crab across the sand. Odd. In this setting she seemed more like a disciplined house cat than a jungle denizen. One thing was for sure, she felt some special connection to Brandon. That picture of them commiserating together a little while ago had not escaped Andrea's curiosity, although she had no idea of what to make of it.

Back at the compound, Brandon inspected the Jumping Viper and paid the Indian twenty Limpiras for the snake. That was more than most Indians made in four days, but it was also golden psychology. Not only was the Indian deliriously happy, he would tell everyone he knew that Don Brandon treated hunters fairly.

Although Andrea didn't want Brandon to know it, his actions also endeared her heart to him. So many people only wanted to take advantage of the Indians. It was a delightful reversal to find someone who wanted to treat them with the dignity they deserved. Without knowing it, or even trying, Brandon was dismantling her resolve to keep a safe distance from him. She knew this was dangerous emotional territory, but she found herself pushing the voice in her head farther and farther away in favor of the voice in her heart.

And then it happened. One night when everyone had gone home, Brandon slipped in the shower and let out a scream. Andrea didn't think. She just rushed headlong into the bathroom to help the man. He was naked except for the injured leg which was still bandaged and wrapped in plastic to try and keep it dry while he washed.

She tried to ignore his maleness, but she became far too aware of the pounding in her heart. In the next moment, their lips met, and all resistance melted in the warm water of the shower. In the next few minutes she became his.

Even as it was happening, one part of her was saying no, but it was no use. The desire was too overwhelming and all she could think of was joining with him and becoming one. And when that happened, the experience far exceeded the physical. It was spiritual. If Andrea would have allowed herself, she would have become transformed to an extension of Brandon. But she couldn't do that, although she came close and there was no denying this moment would change her to some degree forever.

CHAPTER SIX

"Reggie's Revelation"

ANDREA WAS IN A FRUSTRATED STIR THE MORNING FOLLOWING her romantic encounter with Brandon. Goddammit. This is NOT what she came here for. She had a job to do and something like this could serve no purpose except to tangle things up, possibly irreparably.

But there was a problem. When sex is good, as in very good, it's almost overwhelming, overpowering, mesmerizing, hypnotic, and if you aren't careful, it will consume you.

It will take possession of your thoughts, your emotions; you will become an addict, wanting nothing more than to become cocooned within the embrace of that someone who has touched your soul so deeply, so tenderly, with something far beyond the physical, rather, with profound love.

Your lover becomes your teacher because that person, intentionally or not, teaches you things about yourself that you never knew. They make you feel things you have never felt before and think things you have never thought before.

Perhaps this is the description of true love, or is it obsession? Is there a difference? Whatever, the price is control, as in, you are no longer 'in control'. You have relinquished that position to taste the forbidden apple.

Although she tried her best to fight it, over the next several days, Brandon and Andrea's relationship transformed, was reborn into a living being of its own, a capsule into which only the two of them fit. Long lover's talks were certainly involved, but there was also intimacy; an intimacy unlike anything she had ever known or dreamed was possible. One problem was that it was all new, uncharted territory for her. She had never allowed herself to fall in love before.

When Brandon touched her, it was as if electricity coursed through her body, leading directly to her soul. It was delicious candy, but her instinct told her it was also very dangerous. Dangerous, but heaven help her, irresistible.

There was one unexpected side effect. Andrea sensed that the closer she became to Brandon; the more guarded and distant Doc became. The once jovial doctor who wanted to think of nothing but partying suddenly didn't smile so much. He seemed somehow defensive. Did he see her as competition, either consciously or subconsciously? Was he secretly gay? She never saw any signs of that, but anything was possible. She had to admit he had a slightly effeminate appearance. Maybe he was gay and didn't know it.

The whole thing was just too much. It was like a giant warm wave sweeping in from the Caribbean that wanted to consume her. She needed a break. She needed to get away, even if just for a few hours so she could think and sort out a lot of things in her mind.

She picked up her camera and told Brandon she was going for a drive. He looked at her quizzically but said nothing as she bounded down the steps and got into the Jeep, started it and drove away, down the jungle trail toward the main road.

At the main road, she paused for a couple of minutes. She

didn't really know where she wanted to go; whether to turn right, toward town, or turn left, toward Sambala, which was less than two Ks down the main road.

On a whim, she decided to turn left. A little over a kilometer later, she approached the cut-off road to the left which went down to Sambala.

She drove that road in a cloud of dust and closed in on the quaint village. Sambala was for all the world like a transplanted piece of Africa. Most of the population here was black, outnumbering the Amer-Indians at least four-to-one. Men fished for a living in dug-out canoes called 'cayucos' and the women farmed taro root which they called 'Yuca'. The taro root was part of their staple diet. From it they made a type of stew, but they also dried the root, ground it into flour using a wooden mortar and pistol, and from that flour made very large, round, thin tortilla-looking type bread which they cooked by tossing it up on the edge of their thatch roofs.

The hot Honduran sun did the baking for them. Andrea had tasted the tortillas which to her were the epitome of bland. They had absolutely no taste, but the villagers loved them.

The yuca bread was undoubtedly an old African recipe. Likewise, there was African cultural color in this village.

So, she parked the jeep in front of the local 'trucha', a Central American version of a general store, asked the owner if it would be alright to leave the Jeep there for a while, and after conversing with him for a minute, took her camera and began walking through the back streets of Sambala.

It didn't take her long to come to the Temple of The Black Jaguar, which was now boarded up. She snapped a photo of the structure and noticed that someone had pinned an ominous looking straw voodoo doll on the door. Although she couldn't know the exact meaning of it, her guess was, it was a warning that this was an evil place to be avoided.

For the next hour, she roamed the streets of Sambala without thinking about where she might be, just enjoying the abandon of getting away and looking for interesting pictures. She found plenty, and among these simple people, she found easy smiles which she happily returned. She took many pictures of everyday life, women performing every-day chores, but being done in houses with exterior walls made of sticks, designed to let the air flow through easily. A method to deal with the heat of the Honduran north coast.

Just like anywhere else in the world, children here played games, made happy noises. Andrea photographed them. She found it interesting how many symbols there were of pronounced strictly African in origin. Slaves from Africa and other countries had been brought to all parts of the Caribbean in the seventeen hundreds by whoever owned that particular region at the time. In the case of Honduras, it was the Spanish. She wasn't sure what they grew here, but working plantations was the reason for slaves being here.

Now, their language had evolved, mixed, and was a curious combination of Spanish and Swahili or Oromo, their native African languages. It was called Garifuna, and hard to understand by any outsider. Luckily, most of them could also speak enough Spanish to get by, and it was through this medium that Andrea communicated with them.

Her exploration of Sambala was suddenly interrupted when, out the corner of her eye, she noticed that she was being watched.

Someone was doing their best to hide themselves behind the corner of a house and probably wouldn't have been noticed by a less observant person. But Andrea was not that person. She noticed everything. Her training had taught her to do so.

Not being one to beat around the bush, when she finished

taking a picture, she turned and walked directly toward the half-hidden person. She wanted to see what was on their mind. When she got a good look at the reclusive intruder, she was surprised to see it was none other than the disgraced Smoke Jaguar.

He tried to shrink back out of sight, but it was too late. Andrea was swift and too direct.

She walked to within three feet of him and said, "Why are you spying on me?"

"I don't mean no harm," Smoke Jaguar said, obviously frightened. The left side of his head was heavily bandaged from having his eardrum shattered. This was not the imposing figure who stood on the dais of his so-called temple and intimidated his followers by the mere fact of his presence.

"You didn't answer my question," Andrea said menacingly. "Answer me!"

"I jus wondered what you doing wid dat camera."

Andrea turned her head sideways ever so slightly. "I detect a central Caribbean accent. Jamaica?"

"Maybe. Could be," Smoke Jaguar said meekly. He held his hands up in front of his face as if he were afraid Andrea might strike him.

"Uh huh," Andrea pressed. "I'll bet it's an interesting story."

"What story?" Smoke Jaguar asked nervously.

"The truth about why you aren't in Jamaica anymore and instead, here in Honduras trying to scam these poor Indians. I realize that you don't have much of a relationship with truth, so that story would probably be hard to extract. Probably impossible, because I doubt you even know what the truth is."

Smoke Jaguar tried to slowly back away, but it did no good. Andrea was on the attack. "What's your real name, Asshole?" Andrea demanded. "And don't hand me that Smoke Jaguar crap. You know that name was stolen from a Maya chieftain."

Smoke Jaguar hesitated. It was the wrong thing to do. Andrea shoved the camera in his face and snapped a picture of his frightened expression. Then she stepped closer. "Tell me your real name, goddammit! Or I'm going to slap the shit out of you right here in front of everybody, so they can see what a coward you really are. The great 'Smoke Jaguar', getting knocked around by a woman. You think you're ruined now? Wait until that story gets out."

"Reggie." Smoke Jaguar said. He continued to hold his hands close to his face defensively.

"Reggie? Reggie what?"

"Reggie Carlson."

Andrea backed off slightly. "Alright, Reggie Carlson. But I still want to know why you're following me."

"Got noting else to do. No temple anymore. People laugh at me. Don't know how I gwyin to make money, how I gwyin to eat."

"Try getting a job. That's what honest people do."

"In Honduras? It only pay three limps a day."

"Well then, maybe you should take your criminal ass back to Jamaica. It would be three Limpiras of honest, hard earned money, instead of fleecing naïve Indians out of money they can't afford for a false prophet's bullshit. You have no morals, 'Reggie'. I detest people like you."

"Sha. I got morals. Mo than yo man, Lord Brandon Shaw."

By now Andrea had turned and started walking away. Reggie flanked her. She stopped and turned to him. "What do you mean by that?"

Reggie stopped and looked down at the ground. "I cahn't say. Shaw find out I tol you, he kills me, sho."

"You're very lucky he didn't kill you the other day. You just don't know how close you came. That was a stupid thing you did. So…what is it you know? You started this. Be man enough to finish it. I have a suspicion it's the reason you've been following me, so you might as well come clean."

"You tink Shaw so high and mity? He noting but a drogero."

Andrea straightened her back. She was suddenly stiff and on guard. "A drogero? You mean, you're accusing Brandon Shaw of being involved with drugs?"

Andrea stared hard at Reggie. He said nothing, but matched her gaze, unblinking. It was now a game of chicken. She stared hard to see who would blink first. But Reggie was not backing down.

Andrea felt a little weak in the knees and unstable, but she couldn't let Reggie know it. She finally took a deep enough breath that she could say, "That's an easy enough accusation to make without proof. And, we both know, you have reason to want to discredit Brandon."

Reggie slowly shook his head. "I tell de truth. I hate Shaw for real, but dat don't change de fact dat I tell de truth."

"Prove it," Andrea challenged.

"How?" Reggie asked.

"Beats me," Andrea countered. "This is your story. You want me to believe you? You prove what you say. What proof do you have? Proof, Reggie, proof!"

"Fo stahters, how you tink I manage to get the black jaguar from him?"

Andrea blinked. That had always puzzled her. "How?"

Reggie smiled an arrogant smile. "An agreement, to keep me quiet 'bout what I know."

"What?" she said, incredulously.

"I followed him one day straight into de valley of de poppies. Took picture. When he saw picture, we made deal fo him to loan me cat."

A lingering mystery had suddenly been cleared up. But the

revelation was about to overwhelm Andrea. She felt like she might faint. She needed to find a place to sit down before she fell. Reggie saw this and quickly took her arm, then led her over to a bench near the stick house they were adjacent to.

Andrea sat, breathing deeply, holding her chest for a minute. Then she began to gather her senses. Was it true? This man she had fallen in love with? The *first* man she had ever fallen in love with? They had been right all along! "Exactly what did you mean, 'Valley of Poppies'?"

Reggie straightened, triumphantly. "De valley. It not far from here. Dey grow poppies dere. It not de only place, but it be one of de places. I tink the main place."

Andrea looked at Reggie. "You're talking about the kind of poppies that…"

"Dey make hero-wine from dem," Reggie finished. "Dey be a house dere where they manufacture de hero-wine too. A complete operation."

"What was Brandon doing there?"

Reggie held his palms upward. "I dunno. He was talking to some fat guy. He didn't stay long. But he was dere. And its fo sha he's involved. Odewise he wouldn't have made the deal wid me."

"You've got to show me this field," Andrea demanded.

"Oh, hell no!" Reggie said, shaking his head and his hands, and backing up a few steps. "It's too damn dangerous to go up dere. Dey got guys wit guns all ovah de place. Everybody know to go waaay round dat valley!"

Andrea gave Reggie a quizzical look. "What do you mean, 'everybody'? You mean to tell me that everyone around here knows that smack is being manufactured right under their noses and nobody does anything about it? That's insane. I think it's a lot more likely that you're a liar and just making this stuff up about Brandon because you hate him."

"No!" Reggie protested. Then he was quiet for several moments as he pondered something. "I will take you close to the valley, but then, you on you on. I don wan to git caught wit you."

Andrea smiled a wry smile while looking at the defeated Reggie. "Be careful, Reggie Boy," she said. "Your absence of courage is showing…again! Come on, let's get going."

Andrea walked with Reggie, through the narrow dirt streets of Sambala, back to the Jeep, observed by the curious stares of the natives.

They boarded, and Reggie pointed the way. They went back up the dirt trail to the main road, then turned left toward Jutiapa, eastward.

After no more than a few minutes, Reggie pointed to a small, weed covered trail to the right.

Andrea brought the Jeep to a halt and examined the narrow trail. Then she looked at Reggie, who seemed paralyzed with fear. She turned the wheel toward the trail and gently let off on the clutch.

The Jeep inched forward. After going a few yards, they entered thick jungle growth. Andrea booted the Jeep forward a little faster.

They crawled cautiously along the jungle trail for a few hundred yards when suddenly they came to a shiny, new looking metal cattle gate, festooned with warning signs that left nothing to the imagination about the fate of trespassers.

Andrea let the Jeep idle for a minute while she read the signs and weighed the risks. The gate was secured with a chain and lock, and there was a four-foot-high barbed wire fence stretching away to the left and right of the gate, so the Jeep was going no farther.

But was it worth the risk to climb over that gate and proceed by foot?

After thinking it over for a long minute, Andrea decided

yes! She turned the motor off and stepped out of the Jeep. "You coming?" she said to Reggie.

Reggie emphatically shook his head no and sat in the Jeep with his arms crossed and his knees together, all of which was body language that said, fear, bordering on panic. Andrea dismissed him as she grabbed the lanyard of the camera and turned toward the gate. For once in his life, Reggie was stone silent, frozen with angst and terror.

She listened carefully for sounds that might indicate trouble, but all she heard were the calls of exotic birds and what sounded like some howler monkeys in the distance. She climbed over the cattle gate and walked up the narrow, weed covered trail.

After twenty minutes she suddenly came to a valley and a clearing. The valley spread out like a folding paper fan between two mountains. It was perfectly hidden because helicopters would have a rough time trying to fly into here. The insidious valley was filled from one side to the other with poppies, the kind used to make heroin. Andrea snapped several pictures of the scene before her.

To the left, there was a small clapboard house with large shuttered windows. The shutters were propped open wide with sticks, allowing ventilation. She took pictures of this too. As she crept closer, she heard sounds coming from inside the house, but her curiosity pushed her ahead. She silently crept up to the house and peeked through a window.

There, inside, were three men on cots, all snoring loudly. Of course, she thought. It was siesta time, and that is what saved her cheerios at this point. She glanced around the room. She saw modern equipment in this old building. This was definitely where the poppies were being processed into powder.

She had seen enough. She withdrew and headed as fast as she could go, back to the Jeep.

Despite the precariousness of her situation, she had to wipe away tears as she made her way down the trail. If what Reggie had said was true and Brandon knew about this, and worse, was somehow involved in it, her newfound bliss filled world was suddenly imploding in on her. She was at once hurt and angry. Her day of peaceful exploration hadn't turned out the way she had planned at all, and it was breaking her heart.

CHAPTER SEVEN

The Snake Safari

"So...what kind of adventure did you have yesterday?"

Andrea seemed far away, in a daze. But she had to pull herself back and answer Brandon's question. "Oh, I went to Sambala and wandered around, taking pictures of the locals."

"Sounds interesting. Can I see the pictures?"

"What? Oh, no. I don't have a modern camera. I'm still shooting film."

"Film? Good god, girl! No one shoots film anymore. This is the 21st century. Everything is on memory cards these days."

"I know. But the camera was my daddy's, and it's the one he taught me with. Besides, I just think film is more romantic than an electronic chip. There are more subtle hues you can capture."

"And you found subtle hues in Sambala?"

"Not necessarily, but you know what I mean."

"I'm trying to. So, is your dad still alive?"

"No, he passed away. I guess that's one reason why the camera is so special to me. Every time I use it, I think of him."

"Well, I guess I understand heirlooms. It's just that film is so…retro. You ever consider adding to it and getting another camera that's a little more up to date?"

"Not really. You know the old saying, if it ain't broke, don't fix it."

Andrea wanted to move the conversation away from photography, but she was so befuddled at the moment that she wasn't sure where to go.

Suddenly the problem was solved for her by the arrival of an old hard top Jeep that came bouncing up the trail and through the entrance arch, its driver tooting the horn incessantly until he rolled to a stop out by the compound and climbed out. It was a tall Amer-Indian man. Then, two more similar looking men got out of the Jeep with him.

They walked toward the house as Brandon made his way down the stairs. They were dressed in shorts and light, long sleeved shirts which needed washing.

When the driver spotted Brandon, he spread his arms wide, smiled a big smile and said, "Hola Don Brandon! Traigamos regalos!"

Brandon reached the bottom of the steps and walked over to greet the newcomer. With a big handshake and then an 'abraso', a Central American hug, he said, "What do you mean, you're bringing me gifts?"

"It's true!" The man said very proudly. "Yellow beards! I bring you yellow beards, lots of them!"

The fer-de-lance is a true denizen of the jungle. It is large, the average length of an adult being from seven to nine feet. Its venom is duo toxic, containing both neurotoxic and hemotoxic properties. This is a damned if you do, damned if you don't, venom. To treat one toxin is to promote the other.

This fact alone makes its bite fatal almost every time. Adding to the problem, the fer-de-lance has extremely long fangs, making venom delivery very deep into its victim. It has a nasty temper and will frequently charge directly at whatever has inspired its ire. Among the general well advised populous, it is feared and avoided.

Oddly, for some reason, they were one of Brandon's biggest stocks in trade. He had one standing order for all the fer-de-lance snakes he could supply, from a laboratory in Florida. It was a general assumption that the lab was trying to develop a more effective anti-venom to counteract the fatal effects of the fer-de-lance bite. But attempts to gain information about the laboratory had hit a brick wall.

Now, these snake hunters began unloading their Jeep, and Andrea knew a photo op was in the making. She quickly headed into her bedroom to retrieve her camera, then dashed back out onto the veranda where she could watch and take pictures while remaining safely out of the way.

With great caution, the three men continued unloading large cloth bags, each one heavy with its serpent contents. They handled the bags like one would handle dynamite and sat them side by side on the ground in the shade. Brandon watched from a few feet away, his feet spread wide and his arms akimbo. There was a definite expression of satisfaction on his face. Eventually, the men had unloaded close to fifty large bags, as many as the Jeep could possibly carry.

Brandon instructed Pablo to bring a large empty garbage can. Then he addressed the boss hunter. "There's two ways we can do this. I can pin each snake and we can measure it with the measuring box, or you can trust my eye, which is a helluva lot quicker, safer, and more generous."

The hunter spread his hands. "Don Brandon, we have done business for years. I have no problem with your estimates."

Brandon nodded. "Fair enough. Then let's get started." At this point, the hunters all backed off and relaxed because according to the unwritten rule, the cargo was now the responsibility of the buyer. They even accepted cold beers, offered to them by Anna Maria.

Lorenzo untied the cord securing the first bag, laid the bag flat on the ground and ever so carefully, using pliers, grabbed the bottom corner of the bag and slowly lifted it, dumping its unhappy contents on the ground. There were three large fer-de-lance. They were dazed by the light and therefore motionless for a moment. Brandon picked the first one up using long snake tongs. "Six and a half feet!" he said loudly. Suyapa, armed with a yellow legal pad and pen, wrote the number down from her safe position next to Andrea on the veranda. Andrea, meanwhile, was having a field day taking pictures.

Brandon carefully lowered the snake into the large garbage can. Then, quickly, before the snakes had a chance to get their bearings, he took hold of the second one with the tongs. "Eight feet!" he said loudly. Suyapa marked it down, Brandon lowered the reptile into the garbage can with the first snake, then he seized the third snake with the tongs. "Eight feet!" Again, the process was repeated.

After all three snakes from the first bag were safely in the garbage can, Pablo Palma slapped the lid on the can and he, along with one of the hunters who volunteered to help him, lifted the can by its handles and made their way to the back of the compound where a large, oval shaped hole had been dug in the ground and surrounded with cement. Then, they shaded the pit from the hot Honduran sun with a palapa covering.

The pit had a stairway which went down into it from ground level at one end allowing access via a narrow doorway. Pablo and the hunter now used this stairway to gain entrance to the pit and empty the contents of the garbage can. By now the snakes were waking up and becoming more active. So, Pablo and the hunter made a hasty retreat, slamming the pit door securely behind them.

Meanwhile, Lorenzo untied the security rope on the second bag, and duplicated his actions with the first bag by lying it flat on the ground. Brandon didn't like waiting for Pablo. "Lorenzo, get another garbage can so we can work faster while Pablo makes trips to the pit." Lorenzo dashed with amazing speed to the tool shed and returned with an additional garbage can. The process resumed. Lorenzo emptied the bag. This time there were four snakes. Brandon got a grip on the closest one to him. "Six feet!" he shouted out. Suyapa wrote the number down. Snake in can, next snake.

The dangerous process repeated itself with surprising smoothness until all bags were emptied and all the snakes were safely housed in the snake pit. There were close to two hundred large, deadly fer-de-lance. Everybody including Brandon hadn't seen this many fer-de-lance in one place for a long time. The normally hard to impress Don Brandon was in awe.

It was pay day for the hunters, and now that work was done, time for cold beers all around in the breezeway. Beers were produced as were key limes, cut into halves, and salt. It was also a time for a pow-wow.

Brandon addressed the headhunter, who, as it turned out, was named Hector De Alba. They clinked beer bottles together with the salutation, "Salud!" then Brandon got down to the obvious question.

"Hector, I've never seen this many yellow beards except once before in my entire life. Tambien, I'm willing to bet you've never seen this many barba amarillo. So, tell me, my old friend. Where? I need to hear the whole story."

Hector took a deep sip of his Salva Vida before speaking. "Don Brandon. There is something crazy going on in the Mosquitia. The barba amarilla are everywhere. There are not hundreds of them, there are thousands of them. If you want more, we can make another trip."

Brandon thought for a moment. "It sounds to me like a

migration. Nature signals a particular species of animal to move en-mass and suddenly, the whole populous of something just rises up and starts to go somewhere. I saw it once with tarantulas in South Texas years ago. It was at night, raining; the highways were covered with them. When did this start?"

Hector shrugged. "A few days ago."

Brandon sunk into deep thought for a few minutes. "I have a better plan. Let me hire you and your men to work for me."

Hector looked a little surprised, but after thinking it over, nodded agreement.

"Okay, good!" Brandon said with a smile. By now, everybody was gathering around the table in the carport. Beers were opened, chairs were being pulled up close. Now that the snakes were safely tucked away in the pit, somebody let Naja out of her run and she joined the group at the table.

"Here's the plan…a safari, into the Mosquitia." Lorenzo sighed audibly. "Hijole'!" he said, closing his eyes in exasperation.

Brandon continued, addressing Hector. "You and your men will be our guides as well as be working for us."

"A snake safari in the pinche' Mosquitia!" Lorenzo cried out in pain.

Now Brandon addressed his right-hand man. "Lorenzo, quit being a pussy. You've got work to do and you've got to do it fast. We don't have near enough snake boxes and that's going to be the only way to transport a large number of snakes safely.

"If you don't have enough wood, you've got to make a run into LaCeiba and get more. We also need more snake bags. A lot more! Suyapa, get on the phone to that seamstress. What's her name, Diana something? Tell her I need 200 bags and I need them by this afternoon."

"This afternoon?" Suyapa said, surprised.

Brandon thought it over. "Okay, tomorrow afternoon. Tell her I'll pay a bonus for doing it fast. She knows what size to make them. She's been making them for me for years. Pablo, you're going to have to run the compound while we're gone."

Pablo nodded in agreement.

"Alright!" Brandon clapped his hands together. "We've got to go into town and get these vehicles gassed up as well as buy supplies. Make sure the walkie talkies are charged up. Cell phones are going to be worthless in that frigging jungle. It's a safari, boys and girls! We're going on a snake hunt. We leave here day after tomorrow at dawn. Hector, you and your boys help Lorenzo with the box building. We've all got a shit load of work to do."

Everybody finished their beers and rose to go their respective directions. All except Andrea. She was in mild shock at what she had just witnessed. This was a different side of Brandon Shaw that she had not seen before, not even glimpsed before.

He was suddenly the leader, the administrator. Here was the person she had heard stories about in command, at total ease with authority and delegating responsibility.

The next twenty-four hours were a frenzy of activity. Suyapa, who didn't drive, had to hitch a ride into town with Lorenzo to not only fetch the snake bags, but fill a hastily put together shopping list.

Lorenzo had to go to the Atlántida Lumberyard and purchase building supplies for construction of the snake boxes. Then, he and the three hunters worked feverishly cranking out close to a hundred snake boxes which were six inches in depth, by 2 feet wide and 4 feet long with a hinged lid at one end.

Then, they had to make sure to drill enough ventilation holes in the sides of them to keep the interior of the boxes cool, as well as to make sure the captured snakes had plenty of air to breathe.

At last, things began to come together, and the frenzy of activity began to subside. A feeling fell over Jungle Cargo not unlike a pall before the storm. Andrea felt it, but she seemed to be the only one. Something told her this safari into the Mosquitia Jungle was going to hold great danger, but she held the feeling in, kept it to herself. To share it would only bring mocking laughter.

Men like these ate danger for breakfast. It wasn't a matter of putting on a show, trying to be macho. These guys were the reason for the word, 'macho'. They had chosen a lifestyle, or perhaps it had chosen them, where bravery was a prerequisite. After a while, a person can become accustomed to anything, and therein resided the real danger. To forget, even for a split second, just how deadly those fangs are could spell death. She doubted they had forgotten. They had just accepted the fact and made the decision to live with it. It was the stuff campfire tales were made of.

Sleep was impossible for Andrea the night before departure. She tossed and turned and no matter how hard she pressed herself against Brandon, she still couldn't close her eyes. Not until sometime in the wee hours before dawn. At last, sleep pulled its dark, comforting sheet over her.

But it seemed no sooner did she drop off to sleep than she was awakened by the sound of Hector's approaching Jeep. It was dawn. Time to arise and get put together for the grueling trip east into the Mosquitia. Andrea pulled herself out of bed with extreme effort. She felt drugged. Every move was a conscious effort.

Eventually she pulled herself together and went out onto the wide front deck where the girls had already prepared coffee, bowls of fresh tropical fruit, oatmeal and hard-boiled eggs.

Everybody gathered around for a hearty breakfast and happy chatter before the day's journey. There were also last-minute instructions to Pablo and the girls, not that they were necessary. These people knew their jobs and had the professionalism to do them right, whether Brandon was there to crack the whip or not.

The morning repast was happy, upbeat and did not last nearly long enough for Andrea's way of thinking. There was a serious moment when everyone gathered in a circle, held hands and said a prayer, imploring God to watch over their hunt and everyone involved. Then, with a collective "Amen!" they officially began the day.

Before she knew it, luggage was loaded aboard the old blue truck which Lorenzo would drive. Naja was let out of her run and instructed to get in the Jeep with Brandon and Andrea.

The three-vehicle convoy came to life, headed out the front gate, toward the main road; Brandon's Jeep in the lead, followed by Hector, with Lorenzo bringing up the rear.

The early morning air felt cool. Andrea tried to enjoy it. She knew it wouldn't last long. She also hoped her feelings of foreboding would pass. So far, they hadn't.

CHAPTER EIGHT

Surprise in The Jungle

ANDREA SHADED HER EYES FROM THE MORNING SUN AS BEST SHE could, using her visor and her hand. She didn't understand how Brandon could look almost directly into it, though he was wearing dark sunglasses.

Not that it mattered. Nothing did, at the moment. Andrea was so out of it from lack of sleep that she was numb all over.

Besides, she was busy being mad at herself. She had never intended for this to turn into an emotional relationship with this man. She hadn't wanted that. Now, here she was, bouncing down a dusty road straight into a green hell which was against every instinct she had. And at this point, there was nothing she could do to stop it. It was a runaway train and she was on the cow-catcher. How in the world had this happened? She felt vulnerable. Hell, she *was* vulnerable!

It happened because despite all her instincts, inborn and otherwise, there was something completely irresistible about the man next to her. If anyone asked her to describe it in words, she would be incapable, at a total loss. But it was there. And it was powerful. So very powerful. Powerful enough to overwhelm her logic, her instinct for self-preservation. She was completely disarmed, and she didn't like it. Was this to be her destiny? Perhaps it was frustration that brought the burning tears to her eyes. She tried to wipe them away without Brandon noticing.

Four hours of bouncing hell passed. Brandon was pretty deft at dodging potholes, but to dodge one was to hit another head on. Progress was slow, nerve wracking and exhausting. Suddenly a sign appeared announcing that the coastal town of Trujillo was to the left. Brandon took the turn and was followed by the other two vehicles. He picked up his walkie talkie for the first time in hours and announced, "Lunch at Sad Mary's." She should have known something was up when Lorenzo replied over his radio, "Ahorale!" then laughed.

Less than ten minutes later, Brandon pulled over to the curb in front of a cinder block building, painted white. A screen door was all that separated the outside from a slightly darker interior. Andrea could hear women's voices coming from inside, even over the sound of the old blue truck pulling up behind them and then Hector and his crew in their covered Jeep.

Brandon said something unintelligible as he tried to get out of the vehicle. He was stiff from the trip. Naja, who was panting, got out of the Jeep to join her master at his side.

Once everyone had disembarked from their vehicles, the crew walked through the opened screen door into what was known as, Sad Mary's Cafe.

Even before Andrea could adjust to the light, she heard a woman's loud voice say, "Well kiss my old wrinkled up ass, if it ain't goddamned Brandon Shaw!"

"Hello, Mary!" Brandon said in greeting. "How have you been?"

Sad Mary looked to be in her sixties. She was thin, wrinkled, wore a cheap flowered dress and in general appeared to be a hag.

"How the fuck do you think I've been?" she replied. "I'm living in the shit-hole of the world, trying to run a café for a bunch of low life, burned out, illegitimate sons of whores. The closest thing we've got for excitement around here is watching the flies fucking on the tables."

Then Sad Mary turned her attention to Andrea. "Well! Who is this? She looks far too classy for you, Brandon. I'm used to seeing you with burned out old chingas. This one is no whore. She's a lady. Sorry about my fucking language," she said to Andrea. "I'm Mary," she said, extending her hand in greeting.

Andrea shook hands with Mary, although with trepidation.

"Hi, I'm Andrea."

"How did you get caught in this fucker's net?" Mary asked with a wry smile.

"Oh, he isn't all that bad, once you get to know him," Andrea said, glancing over at Brandon.

Mary cackled. "Oh shit! I guess I know what that means. Well, come on in and get comfortable, all of you. What'll it be today?"

"I think a better question is, what have you got that's good to eat?" Brandon asked as tables were arranged and everybody sat.

"We've got a pot of pork stew on," Mary said. "No potatoes, the bastard delivery truck didn't come. Guess the driver is high again. Anyway, I put some yuca in it. It ain't too bad. It'll probably give Andrea here the shits if she ain't used to Honduran food."

"Well," Brandon said with slight resignation. "I guess I'll try some. I'm hungry enough to eat just about anything." Everyone else nodded agreement and Mary disappeared into the kitchen. Andrea immediately locked eyes with Brandon. He looked at her knowingly and said in a low voice, "Kind of a shock to the system, isn't she?"

Andrea responded by raising one eyebrow, then looked down at Naja, lying at Brandon's feet, peacefully panting like a house dog. It occurred to Andrea that everything which surrounded her was foreign to anything she was familiar with. She was in the café of an obscene woman who was probably to some degree crazy, with a man she didn't really know who had a three-hundred-pound jaguar reposed like a house cat at his feet. She needed to take a deep breath and excused herself to step outside for a minute.

Despite the unforgivable foul mouth of Sad Mary, the traveling crew made it through lunch. The stew wasn't bad, albeit Andrea didn't have much of an appetite. Whether that was due to the road from hell, this bizarre situation, or Mary's unbelievably foul mouth, Andrea wasn't sure. All she did know for sure was that she wanted this safari to be over with. When they were back in the Jeep, and on the road, Brandon offered an explanation about Sad Mary.

"I'm not sure where Mary is originally from, or how she wound up in such an ungodly place as Trujillo. There's a lot of ex-patriots in this country and they all have their own reasons for being here. Anyway, they say Mary used to be a knock your hat in the creek, beautiful and cultured woman. That's hard for me to imagine. Be that as it may, Trujillo is a port, and all the banana ships used to come into Trujillo to load. Apparently, there was a Louisiana Cajun coon-ass on one of those ships that Mary fell head over heels in love with. From what I've been told, the romance was red hot, torrid, whatever you want to call it. Mary was completely in love with this character.

"Then, Standard Fruit started porting farther up the coast, at LaCeiba. It's not all that far from LaCeiba to Trujillo, but Mister Coon Ass never came to see Mary when his ship was in port; abandoned her. Cold as ice. Maybe that road from LaCeiba to here was just too rough, even for love.

"The story goes that she fell into melancholy and had a

nervous breakdown. That's when the radical change began. What you see today is what her grief did to her."

Andrea looked at Brandon incredulously.

Brandon glanced over at Andrea's expression.

"What? You don't think a broken heart can twist you like that?"

"What kind of a timeline are we talking about?"

"I don't know. Forty years, maybe."

"Good Lord," Andrea mused. "She threw away an entire lifetime pining for one man?"

"True love, my dear. True love."

"Yes…but…"

"But what?"

Andrea shook her head and returned her gaze to the road ahead. "Never mind," she said in resignation. Andrea wondered, was Sad Mary a warning?

Two more hours passed and then something appeared ahead that sent chills through Andrea. A wall of trees stood before them that marked the boundary to the Mosquitia Jungle. The wall was made stark because loggers had cut all the trees right up to where the jungle was protected against foresting by the Honduran government.

What had been a virgin forest up to that invisible border was now a denuded, ruined heap of discarded branches, turning brown in the sun all the way to the horizon in both directions. Tree stumps stood as reminders.

Then the jungle. The road they must traverse entered what appeared to be a dark green tunnel. Brandon brought the Jeep to a halt for a minute while Andrea snapped a few photos.

Then, he let off the clutch and the Jeep moved forward until it entered the narrow opening through the trees. The light of day disappeared behind them. Suddenly, they were in a shadowy world, a close world. A world much too closed in for Andrea's liking.

Progress slowed to a crawl here. Not only was the passageway like a green tunnel, but gnarled roots crawled along the surface of the ground and made every foot of forward travel a living hell. Adding to it, there was a pervasive musty smell. This was not like the jungle surrounding Jungle Cargo at all. Andrea decided, if she survived this, she would never fear hell again; she had already been there.

Not only could she hear the whine of the Jeep more loudly here, but she could hear the engines of the other two vehicles behind them, groaning away as they negotiated every gnarled, creepy root that crossed the so-called road.

An hour later, Andrea was near her wit's end, trying to hang on for dear life against the constant, never ending crawl across torturous surface roots. Then suddenly, mercifully, the road smoothed out. The roots had been removed and five minutes later they came to a very large clearing in the middle of the jungle.

There, on the right side of the road was an incredible, unbelievable sight. There was a single-story hotel, painted white as snow with a grand entrance right in the center of the front and wide steps leading to a blue tiled landing. A sign painted on the wall above the frieze announced: JUNGLE INN. Andrea gasped. She could hardly believe her eyes. She thought for a minute that the heat had finally gotten to her and she was hallucinating.

And standing there, at the center of the landing, with a broad smile on his face was a very short, as in somewhere between a midget and a dwarf, man, deformed and scarred from the effects of leprosy. His name was Didier Marin, and he was the owner/proprietor of The Jungle Inn. He was neatly dressed in a beige tropical suit with jacket. He spread his short arms and stubby fingers wide in hospitable greeting. "Brandon Shaw! I knew you would be here. I made a bet with Hector when he left here that he would not return alone. I am so glad to see you. It has been too long!"

"Hello, Didier," Brandon said, offering the small man a hug in greeting. Didier turned his attention to Andrea. "And who might this lovely vision be?"

Brandon introduced Andrea with pride. "Didier, I want you to meet Andrea Granger. She's working with me now, at the compound."

Didier offered his stubby hand to Andrea. "So very honored to meet you, beautiful lady. I must say, you look a bit haggard from your journey. Please come inside and accept some refreshment, on the house of course. Your rooms are ready and waiting."

"Glad to meet you, Didier. Rooms ready and waiting?"

"Of course. I had no doubt Brandon Shaw would be here, so I had everything prepared in advance!" Didier smiled broadly. At that moment, the rest of the convoy arrived and pulled up in front of the hotel. Weary travelers piled out of vehicles.

Didier did a quick visual scan. "Oh my! Everyone looks exhausted. Come! Everybody, to the bar we must go. I have a very special exotic drink sure to please and erase the effects of that ungodly road. It's my own concoction. I call it, 'Jungle Juice'! I won't tell you everything that's in it, but a hint is, there is a lot of very good, dark rum!"

Didier looked at Naja who was plastered to Brandon's side, then reached down to pet her. "And for you, young lady, we have a big pan of cool water, and what do you want to bet my chef can find a fat leg of tapir for your dinner? We aim to please everybody!" Didier was genuinely happy to see the entourage, and it showed. He hurried about, giving instructions to various uniformed wait staff, clapping his short hands together.

Andrea looked at Brandon and said quietly, out the corner

of her mouth, "Full of surprises, huh Bwana!" Brandon laughed softly as they followed Didier.

Andrea began to feel better as the afternoon gave way to evening. A couple of Didier's Jungle Juices certainly helped, as did a sojourn to the well-appointed-spotlessly clean room where she washed off the day with a long hot shower. She was in mild shock to find this place so deep in the jungle. And it certainly wasn't how she thought her day would end. She saw hammocks slung in trees, lots of sweat and mosquitos, extreme discomfort. It was hard to believe her good fortune. Why hadn't Brandon told her? Oh well, never mind!

It made no logical sense, but as the revitalizing water cascaded over her hair and face, she found herself not caring what made sense. She was just profoundly grateful for such a jewel of an oasis in this tangle of a jungle.

Refreshed and dressed in a light cotton blouse and white shorts, she returned to the bar which doubled as the dining area. She found Brandon and Didier sitting at a table deep in conversation, but relaxed and laughing. Both men rose at Andrea's approach. Brandon offered her a cushioned, rattan chair.

Next to them, tables had been pushed together to form a long dinner table, which was covered with a white tablecloth and was at present being dressed in expensive china and silverware for dinner. Their host was planning on serving dinner family style.

One by one, Hector and the other hunters emerged from refreshing themselves in their rooms. And now, in this eleventh hour, Brandon excused himself to go take a quick shower. Suddenly Andrea found herself seated alone with Didier Marin. He smiled across at her. "Would you like another Jungle Juice, or would you prefer to switch horses and go with the amusing house wine?"

"Wine?" Andrea mused. "You have wine? Why am I not

surprised? Yes, wine, please." Didier motioned to the waiter who retreated to the kitchen to fetch the bottle of wine and glasses.

Andrea addressed her host. "Didier… I cannot begin to tell you what a shock and wonderful surprise arriving here today has been. I will tell you without hesitation, I think the Jungle Inn is a thing of fantasy stories."

Didier smiled broadly. "Thank you, dear lady. It took me twenty-five years to get this hotel to the point you see it at now. When I started, this spot was nothing but jungle, just like everything you see around you."

"But how…?"

"Little by little. Needless to say, everything had to be brought in here from somewhere. It was a dream against all odds. A labor of love. A defiance of logic. There used to be a colony of lepers that were banished to this jungle. That included my parents. They're all dead now, disease, old age, other causes. But there were also missionaries. They taught me to read. I got my hands on books such as encyclopedias and even some magazines. I saw a hotel in one of the travel magazines and knew in the blink of an eye that's what I wanted to do with my life."

"Amazing," Andrea said. "Just…absolutely amazing. Stunning, actually. I mean, the desire is one thing; but to actually accomplish such a thing…*here!*"

The waiter arrived with the wine, a 1969 Cabernet. He opened the bottle and stayed faithful to ritual by offering Didier a sample to taste. Then he poured.

"Of course, this will be much better after it's had a few minutes to breathe," Didier said. "But, here's to your health." He hoisted his glass and clinked with Andrea.

Behind the Jungle Inn was a broad, flag stoned patio. This is where Naja had been offered her supper. Now, she could be heard happily gnawing away on the tapir leg. She was content. Didier paused to listen to her for a moment as bones were crunched into paste. "Kind of makes you glad she's on our side, doesn't it?" It was good for a relaxing laugh, just as Brandon approached them, fresh from his shower. He had been the one they were waiting on. Now everyone moved to the dinner table and the evening meal began in earnest.

Dinner was sumptuous; first came a garden salad, straight out of the Jungle Inn garden. In the place of lettuce, which was difficult to grow in the heat, there was kale, and plenty of garden-fresh tomatoes, and radishes, mushrooms and a home-made salad dressing made of olive oil, parsley, egg-whites, and dry mustard, also spiced with garlic.

The entrée was slow roasted wild boar, cooked over an open fire. Didier's chef had done something to remove the wild taste. On the side there were ripe plantains baked and made to taste more like sweet potato, and sautéed mushrooms, obviously grown here. Dessert was flan, with a dash of coffee liqueur. By the time Andrea laid her napkin on the table, she felt as if she had just visited a five-star restaurant.

She laid her head back. "Good Lord, Didier, you are a miracle maker! This was fabulous! And, forgive me for repeating myself, but here, so deep in the jungle. I'm convinced that you have a genie in a bottle here somewhere. Thank you for a fabulous evening."

"Your praise has made the effort my pleasure," Didier said. "But now, we simply must cap this all off with an after-dinner cordial." Before Andrea could politely refuse, the waiter, whom by now she had learned was known as Pepe, appeared with glasses and a bottle of Presidente Brandy.

For music, there were the night sounds of the jungle. A myriad of tree frogs brought the darkness to life with a thousand songs. The nocturnal orchids opened and released their delicate perfume. It was a seduction that lulled Andrea away from her dread and foreboding, and even her weariness. Or so she thought.

The brandy managed to do it. It finished off what the Jungle Juice, earlier in the evening, had begun. She was in the bag and found it difficult to remain awake. The table conversation became a blur and soon she felt Brandon's arms beneath her back and knees as he lifted her to carry her gently to the room. She was too out of it to be embarrassed. She melted into his arms as he made his way down the tiled corridor, then opened the door and placed her ever so gently on the bed.

He slipped off her shoes and covered her with a sheet, then retreated and left her there alone to fall gracefully into slumber.

She slept the sleep of the innocent. But sometime during the night, there came a dream. She felt as if she awoke from a peaceful sleep and Brandon was not there. Hearing soft sounds, she went to the screened window and peered out. Brandon was there, in the hotel garden, sitting on a picnic table. Naja was at his side, but then on closer inspection, she thought she could make out the form of another jaguar there in the moonlight; a rosetted jaguar, in the shadows. It was hard to make out the forms because the area was illuminated only by the moon and that light was filtered through the jungle canopy.

As she continued to watch this bizarre scene, more jaguars began to arrive in the garden of the Jungle Inn until at last, there had to be a dozen of them, and they all surrounded Brandon as if he was Buddha. He spoke to each of them.

She couldn't make out what he was saying, but the mesmerizing thing was that all the jaguars were listening intently. He gently stroked each of their heads. One of them hopped up on the table beside Brandon and laid down.

"Ugh!" Andrea thought. She should have left that brandy alone! This was too much, even for a dream. The worst part was it seemed so real. But then, didn't all dreams seem real?

She returned to the bed and faded into blackness. When she wakened again, Brandon was sleeping beside her. She slid her arm across his chest and snuggled tight against him. A small smile found its way to her lips as she drifted off. How silly, she thought. Brandon surrounded by wild jaguars in the dead of night. Really!

CHAPTER NINE

The Omen Comes True

ANDREA AWOKE TO THE SOUNDS OF MEN WORKING IN FRONT OF the hotel. Brandon had apparently slipped out of bed to go direct the hunters, leaving Andrea to rest for as long as possible. He knew the events of yesterday had been very taxing on her. She dressed quickly, and followed the noise, driven by her curiosity.

Hector and his hunters were off-loading all the wooden snake boxes and stacking them beside the truck. The plan was, as boxes were filled, they would be placed back onto the truck.

Thus completed, it was time to take the morning break and gather 'round in the combination bar/dining area for a delightful breakfast of coffee, fresh fruit, fried eggs and salsa, sausage patties and instructions from Brandon Shaw about the layout for the day.

Two men would stay with the truck for correct packing and handling of the snake boxes as they were filled.

One person would drive the Jeep and essentially be the runner, going back and forth from the hunting area, transporting filled snake bags to the truck. Everyone else would be in the field, hunting and catching. But they needed at least two more men. This problem was simply handled because several Mosquitia Indians had shown up at the hotel when they heard of the arrival of Brandon Shaw and Company. Brandon left the selection of which two Indians to Lorenzo, since Lorenzo spoke a little Mosquitia and Brandon did not.

Then he turned to Andrea. "I have a surprise for you," he said and walked over to the Jeep where he withdrew a pair of very high leather boots. He handed them to Andrea.

"I hope they fit," he said.

Andrea took the boots, looked at them.

"Where did you get these?" she asked.

"They belonged to somebody else...a long time ago. Someone who didn't want them...didn't want me. If you're going with us today, they aren't an option. Please put them on."

Andrea went to the nearest chair and slipped off her tennis shoes, then tried on the first boot. It felt good. Then she donned the other. She returned to Brandon.

"Thank you. I think I'm ready."

Brandon nodded, but said nothing. At this point, he walked over to Naja and looked her in the eye. "Girl, you've got to wait here."

Andrea watched in amazement. It was as if Naja knew exactly what Brandon was saying.

And when he walked away to get in the Jeep with Andrea, Naja didn't move a muscle. She just sat on her haunches and watched him depart.

Andrea wished it was her staying at the hotel instead of, or with Naja. She had never been very fond of snakes, try as she might. And suddenly, here she was, going into the valley of the fer-de-lance, one of the deadliest snakes in the world. Glory! She hoped she would be able to tell her grandkids about this one.

They had barely driven two minutes away from the hotel

when suddenly Brandon slammed on the brakes and bailed out of the Jeep.

He quickly grabbed his capture-bag and snake-hook, then walked at a fast pace a few yards ahead of the vehicle. Andrea tried to see what Brandon was seeing. Crossing the dirt road in front of them was a huge fer-de-lance. It was at least as big around as her leg. This is what they had come here for.

Brandon approached the snake as carefully as possible.

By now Hector's Jeep had pulled up behind them and the hunters had bailed out to watch.

Brandon deftly maneuvered the snake hook beneath the snake and started to pull it toward the capture-bag when suddenly the snake came to life and struck, missing Brandon by scant inches. Brandon still managed to get the bag over its head, then worked the rest of the snake's body into the capture bag. He twisted the bag tight. The first snake of the hunt was theirs. Everybody cheered. Everybody that is, except Andrea. She was hanging on to the top of the windshield frame staring in awe. Brandon had come scant inches from being bitten, and it didn't seem to faze him. "Business as usual!"

One of the hunters took a holding bag over to Brandon so he could transfer the snake from the capture bag, which essentially was a large dip net made for fishing, with the net removed and a cloth bag affixed in place of the net. The transfer was made by slipping a holding bag over the top of capture bag, then untwisting the capture bag and pouring the contents from the capture bag into the holding bag. Then the holding bag would be twisted tight, so the contents could not move while a nylon lanyard was tied at the top of the holding bag.

But Andrea didn't notice any of this. She was paralyzed with fear which had seized her after seeing how close Brandon came to being bitten.

She held on, white knuckled to the Jeep and stared straight

ahead.

After Brandon had made the transfer, he turned and looked at Andrea with a big smile on his face, until he saw her expression. His smile evaporated, and he moved quickly toward the passenger side of the vehicle to see what was wrong.

By now, Andrea was shaking uncontrollably.

"I can't do this," she said with a quavering voice. "I thought I could, but I can't. That snake almost killed you. If it had struck at me, I wouldn't know what moves to make to avoid being bitten. This is crazy. I'm out of my element. Please take me back to the hotel."

Brandon nodded and told Lorenzo he would be back in a couple of minutes. Then he boarded the driver's side of the Jeep and turned back toward the hotel.

He didn't say so aloud, but he was relieved that Andrea wanted to spend her day in the safety of the hotel. He knew that this enterprise was dangerous, even for him. He grabbed the walkie-talkie and sent a message ahead to Didier. "We're coming back to the hotel. Andrea has hit exhaustion. Too dangerous for her here."

A couple of minutes later, Brandon pulled up in front of the wide stairway entrance to the JUNGLE INN. Didier and Naja were there on the landing, anxiously waiting. Brandon helped Andrea up the steps and through the main concourse toward the bar seating area.

"I'll have Alberto make a nice herbal tea that will help settle her nerves," Didier said.

Andrea sank into one of the cushioned rattan seats and put her face in her hands. Brandon squatted down beside her, rubbed her back with his broad hand for a moment. "Just take it easy. You chill here, and don't let Didier talk you to death."

He paused for a few moments. Then, "You going to be alright?"

Andrea nodded yes. The chef arrived with the hot tea which she gladly sipped.

Didier said, "Don't worry about a thing. We're going to take good care of her. Go do what you've got to do."

Brandon nodded while still looking at Andrea, "Yeah...well the guys are waiting for me. I really shouldn't leave them alone..."

Andrea looked at him imploringly. "I'll be fine," she said. "But can you leave me a walkie-talkie, so I can know what's going on?"

"Didier has one. He'll loan you his."

"Of course," Didier said.

"Thank you," Andrea said with a weak smile.

"Well, okay. Keep that walkie talkie close. If I'm needed, I'll be here before you can blink." Brandon said, still slightly worried.

He kissed her on the head and retraced his steps back to the Jeep, which was still idling. A moment later he was on his way back to the hunting area.

Andrea heard the Jeep fading back into the jungle as she sipped her hot tea.

Didier sat in a chair across from her. "I'll stay for a moment, if you don't mind, in case you need to talk."

"That snake nearly killed Brandon and he didn't think a thing of it," she said softly, over the rim of her teacup.

Didier said nothing now. He wanted Andrea to talk. It would be the most therapeutic thing for her. But it appeared that is all she was going to say, unless he primed the pump somewhat.

"Brandon Shaw is a remarkable man," Didier said. "I have known him for many years. I have never seen him show fear. Men like Brandon don't know the meaning of the word, what few of them there are."

Andrea shook her head. "Doesn't he realize that dying is

very final? It's eternal. It means the end of life as we know it? Death is...THE END! Finis! Kaput! No more! Good heavens, there must be some awe, some respect for that. Some... reverence, some kind of fear." Her voice faded.

"Maybe it's just not in his DNA."

"Oh, come on, Didier. Doesn't that sound a little campy, even to you?"

"You don't think that genes contribute to who you are? What you are?"

Andrea was silent a long moment while she thought about Didier's words.

"I guess I never thought about it from that angle," she confessed.

"Everyone is driven to some degree by their ancestors, or at least influenced. I don't know you, but I would be willing to wager that you have your grandmother's eyes, or you cook pancakes the way she cooked pancakes, or..."

"Okay, I get the point," Andrea said. "So, you're telling me that Brandon descends from a long line of maniacs?"

Didier laughed. "Not necessarily maniacs. Probably more like bullfighters. I'd bet if you investigated his family history, you would find at least one person somewhere in that family tree who was known for their courage."

Andrea sighed. "Well, I was looking forward to a day of getting some really spectacular photographs. I really blew it."

Didier smiled. "You didn't blow it. Take today to gather your thoughts and try again tomorrow. You're probably still exhausted from the trip. It isn't very pleasant from LaCeiba to here, Lord knows."

Andrea's eyes widened. "Tomorrow? I thought this would be completed and we would be on the way back by tomorrow."

Didier shook his head. "No way. Brandon and his men will work slowly. That's the only way to work safely. The more one rushes when manipulating death, the greater the chance of an accident. It's dangerous enough as it is. You'll be here tomorrow."

Andrea took a deep breath, then sipped her tea. She leaned back in the chair and crossed her legs. That was the first time she had a chance to take a good look at the boots Brandon had given her. "Nice boots," she said. "Dusty, but like new."

Didier smiled knowingly. "They belonged to someone else several years ago. Another woman that Brandon brought here."

Andrea met Didier's gaze. "He brought someone else here?"

"It was the last time we had one of these bizarre migrations, or whatever they are," Didier said. "But…she was different. She didn't have a chance of fitting in. She was bouncing off the walls the whole time they were here. I think her idea of wild adventure was a trip through the mall."

Andrea smiled. "So, what happened?"

"Brandon reached his limit. He called in a Medivac helicopter. Claimed she was having a nervous breakdown. Had her taken out of here. The last any of us saw of her was flying out of sight over the treetops.

"Brandon never looked back, never mentioned her again, just returned to business as usual. With you, it's different. He cares about you. A blind man could see it."

"How do you know?"

"It's the way he tended to you when you returned a little while ago. He fawned over you. Made sure you were all right before he took off. I think he loves you."

Andrea's mouth curled into a smile. "You really think so?"

Didier nodded yes. "I'd bet on it. I, Madame, am an observer of life. In a place like this, you learn to be very astute. He loves you."

She thought for a minute.

"I've let him down." She frowned. "I've got to get a grip

and try again. I just had a panic attack. I need to realize that those men know what they're doing. I'll be okay as long as I stay in the Jeep."

Andrea began to pull herself together. Hearing that Brandon might love her gave her new resolve.

At that moment, Andrea heard Hector's Jeep approaching. It was the driver bringing in the first load of filled snake bags. Andrea walked to the front to observe the operation and to snap a few photos.

A snake box was laid on the ground just behind the Jeep and opened. Snake tongs were used to grab the top of a cloth snake bag in the Jeep, and that bag was lowered into the box. Generally, the bag was pushed farther back in the box via use of the tongs, and a second bag placed beside it, all depending on how full the bag(s) were.

Then the lid was closed, secured and placed on the truck. The operation was repeated until the Jeep had been emptied. Always and always, tongs were used to handle the bags when moving them from the Jeep to the boxes.

When the driver got in the Jeep to return to the hunting area, Andrea slid in on the passenger side, smiled and in her best Spanish said, "Can I hitch a ride with you back to where Brandon is?"

The driver nodded, and they drove away. Didier, standing on the hotel landing, watched them go and said low, to himself, "I think Brandon has met his match this time!"

Back at the hunting ground, Brandon was very surprised to see Andrea. As she got out of Hector's Jeep and into Brandon's Jeep, she winked at him, smiled and said,

"I couldn't stay away!" Brandon smiled a half smile but was too busy being on the lookout to give her the attention he wanted. The situation was just plain dangerous. There were so many snakes on the move that it wasn't necessary to go looking for them. It was more like intercept them as they passed by.

In some cases, the reptiles were so bent on trying to go wherever it was that nature was dictating them to go, that all that was necessary to catch them was place the capture bag in front of them and they would crawl into it. Then it was just a matter of transferring them from the capture bag into a holding bag and placing the bag in the Jeep. The repetition was almost boring, and therein was the danger. Relaxing the guard, even for a split second could be deadly.

Adding to the problem was that the heat was oppressive. And here, among the trees and jungle canopy, there was no breeze. The danger of overheating was extreme, so it was necessary for everyone to drink water almost constantly and keep a wet towel around their neck. Their shirts were drenched in perspiration. Except that is for the Indians. They were born into this heat and acclimated to it. Being shirtless also probably helped.

After what seemed like forever, it was lunchtime. Everyone loaded up and headed for the hotel, which was less than fifteen minutes away. Andrea was struck by the attitude of these men. When they broke for lunch, it was if they were breaking from mowing a lawn or some other such mundane job. The irony was not lost on her.

Lunch was not rushed. It was not served family style either. The tables were separated, and several electric fans positioned around the dining area to move the air. Lots of water with lime juice was served over ice to cool everybody down. This wasn't just lunch, it was also the siesta hour, and nothing would happen, no matter how important or pressing until after 2:00 p.m. This was Honduras. One simply did not vacate the protocol of a nap following lunch.

When everyone was finally rousing after the siesta hour, an Indian named Chucon showed up to replace his brother who was needed at home. Chucon was eager but had not been trained. He also seemed very young and maybe a little naïve.

Be that as it may, everyone piled into vehicles and headed for the hunting grounds.

Things went according to rote for a while. A snake would be found, cornered, urged one way or the other into the capture bag, then transferred into a holding bag which would be twisted tight, then tied with a nylon cord.

The bag would then be placed carefully into the Jeep, via use of long tongs and attention would turn to the next capture.

Andrea had to admit to herself that the longer she watched this process, the more science she realized there was to it. It was dangerous, yes. But the amount of danger really was being minimized with the amount of care that was being taken. Then suddenly, without warning, that tenuous security was shattered.

The tragedy happened when the new Indian helper, Chucon, was loading a bag into the Jeep.

He was using the tongs, as instructed, but he hadn't squeezed the handle tightly enough. The bag slipped loose and landed on the ground behind the Jeep. In that single moment, without thinking, the Indian reached down to grab the top of the bag. And in that one split second, the furious fer-de-lance inside the bag saw the shadow and struck. His fangs pierced through the cloth bag and sank deep into the left forearm of Chucon.

Chucon had time to scream and spring back from the bag. He said, "I've been stung!" in his native language and held his bleeding arm. Although Brandon did not understand Mosquitia, it didn't take an interpreter to know what had happened.

Brandon rushed to his Jeep and grabbed the first aid kit, plus the anti-venom in the cooler. Chucon was sobbing, holding his arm and babbling in Mosquitia,

"Am I going to die?"

Brandon started preparing vials of anti-venin and

administering them, but the bite was deep in the left arm. A worse location could not have been imagined. Within a couple of minutes, Chucon keeled over, comatose. It was all so quick.

"Must have got him in a vein," Brandon muttered as he worked feverishly to get more anti-venin in the young Indian.

It was no use and Brandon knew it, even as he worked furiously, hoping against hope. Within minutes, Chucon quit breathing. Attempting mouth to mouth or anything else would be useless.

The jungle had exacted its fee this day. Brandon looked at the dead boy as if it were his own son, then sagged down to sit on the ground while he collected his thoughts and emotions.

Andrea was in shock. She simply couldn't get her head around this. A young man had died right in front of her eyes.

Lorenzo, Hector and the other hunters gathered around.

Brandon pulled himself together enough to instruct the men to load the Indian boy into his Jeep. The hunt was over. Everyone was to return to the hotel.

Minutes later, the two Jeeps pulled up in front of the Jungle Inn. The other Indian that had been helping on the blue truck saw his stricken brother and began to wail. Didier and other personnel including maids at the hotel showed up on the landing, saw what had happened and reacted.

After a few minutes here, the next step was to go to the Indian village and take the boy home. It was not something Brandon was looking forward to. He told Andrea of the necessary trip and asked her if she would rather wait at the hotel. She looked Brandon straight in the eye and said, "How dare you ask me that. Let's go to the village."

Everybody went, even Didier.

The capture Jeep was emptied and loaded with passengers. Chucon's brother rode in Brandon's Jeep, cradling the body of his dead brother and chanting something in Mosquitia that Brandon assumed to be a type of prayer.

The pair of Jeeps slowly wound their way along a narrow trail which led to the village.

As the jungle huts came into sight, they found a gathering of villagers standing together, waiting for them. This included the old man who would be considered the chief, Tinto, and he spoke Spanish.

Brandon dismounted and approached Tinto, saying, "There's been a horrible accident."

"Yes," Tinto replied. "The forest has told us." He walked over to the young Indian, now dead and placed his hand on the boy's head.

"He was a good boy, but always careless."

Brandon and Andrea said nothing. She was still sitting in the Jeep. Tinto turned and walked back to Brandon. "You will be at the ceremony tonight?"

Brandon nodded. "Of course, I will. I think most of us will if that's all right?"

Tinto raised his hand. "The spirit of Chucon will be gladdened." Then he signaled to some village men to collect the body of Chucon and take it to a special hut.

The two Jeeps returned to the Jungle Inn.

Brandon gathered everyone around him in the bar. "This hunt is over," he said. "Lorenzo, tie down all the boxes, filled and unfilled, to that truck very tightly. We'll attend the funeral ceremony tonight, but tomorrow, we pull out at dawn. We're going home. One death is too many. I'm sick to death of this fucking business. Goddammit! I've got to get out before I go crazy."

It was only then that Brandon looked up and saw a rather tall, slender, Hispanic man sitting at another table, quietly watching him. The man wore a broad brimmed hat and smoked a small, dark cigar.

Brandon squinted slightly, trying to focus. "Antonio? Antonio Munoz? Is that you?"

"It is I!" the man said and rose to walk over to Brandon and shake hands.

"What the hell are you doing here? I mean, all the way from Copan?" Brandon asked.

"Brandon Shaw!" Antonio said with a smile, shaking Brandon's hand. "Didier told me you were here. I came to see you. But, uh…it seems the timing is bad, eh?"

Brandon shook his head in defeat. "We lost one today. Should have never happened. I've got to get out of this business. I'm sick of it."

Andrea, watching from the sidelines, raised her eyebrows. This was the first time she had heard Brandon express discontent. She smiled inside. It was great news. She rose and walked to where Brandon and Antonio stood. At her approach, Antonio spotted her, then Brandon. "Ah! Antonio, let me introduce Andrea Granger. She works for the company but is with me at Jungle Cargo for a spell."

Antonio took Andrea's outstretched hand. "Encantado!" he remarked. The three sat down at the nearest table.

"What happened out there?" Antonio inquired.

"Young Indian boy, no experience, made a mistake. With the yellow beards, one mistake is sometimes all you get. Snake got him in the left forearm. He was gone in a matter of minutes."

Antonio shook his head. "Tragic. I am sorry."

Brandon looked away for a minute, then back at Antonio. "Wait. You said you came here to see me. Any special reason, or you just knocking around the jungle?"

"There's a lot of activity here in the Mosquitia. Archaeologists have discovered a huge Mayan city which they have named 'Lost City of the Monkey God', although I doubt seriously that's what the Maya called it. This one dates back about fifteen hundred years."

"Wow!" Brandon said. "I didn't think their florescent period went back that far."

"Not only did it go back that far, but there is evidence that this whole damn jungle may be interlaced with ruins."

"Really?"

"Brandon, I can see that you have your hands full tonight, but I heard you say something about going back home tomorrow."

"Yeah, I've pretty much had it."

Antonio looked very serious. "Don't go before you see something. I want to take you to the Lost City of the Monkey God with me."

Brandon looked confused. "For what possible reason? What's so important?"

Antonio stared Brandon in the eye. "I'd rather not say. You need to see for yourself."

Brandon stared at Antonio a long moment, then looked over at Andrea. "Can you go with Lorenzo in the truck?"

Andrea looked sternly at Brandon.

"Like hell! I'm not riding back to Jungle Cargo in a truck filled with snakes. Let Lorenzo handle that. He's perfectly capable. I'm going with you to the Lost City of the Monkey God."

Brandon turned to Antonio "Is it okay if she goes?"

Antonio nodded yes. "It's okay with me. But, as you know, there are many secrets hidden within the darkness of the jungle, Jefe. She may learn more than you want her to."

Later, in their room, preparing to go to the ceremony for Chucon, Andrea tried to dig deeper.

"What did Antonio mean with that little poetic speech he made about, 'Many secrets are hidden within the darkness of the jungle'? And, 'She might learn more than you want her to'?"

"Who knows," Brandon said as he buttoned his shirt. "Antonio has always been given to believing in the occult; spirits, ancient Mayan spirits, in particular. One time I was visiting Copan, in Western Honduras. That's where I met Antonio, he was my guide. Anyway, it was hot as hell. Temperature was in the 90s, no breeze; I was sitting on an old stone stairway trying to get my breath. Antonio said, 'I'll get us some breeze here to cool you off'. I said, 'How?' He said, 'Just watch,' and he began to whistle."

Andrea laughed. "Whistle? How did that help?"

"Well, it was the strangest thing. A minute or so later, the treetops started moving, gently at first, then they started really swaying, being blown around. This nice breeze came and blew for a couple of minutes, cooling us off. Then, it died down. It got my attention. Actually, it scared the crap out of me."

After thinking about it for a minute, Andrea said, "And what do you think about 'spirits', Brandon?"

Brandon glanced over at her but said nothing. Then, "Let's go to the Indian village and get this over with."

Andrea looked at Brandon without saying anything. But the look in her eye said that somehow, she believed the story, and it confirmed her suspicion about Antonio.

Later, at the Indian village, both Jeeps arrived with the entire entourage to pay their respects.

They found a large bonfire in the center of the compound with a circle of people surrounding the fire, doing a kind of dance and chant.

Andrea did not understand at first that the body of Chucon was in that fire, being cremated. The whole thing was very disturbing to her and she held tight to Brandon's arm without letting go.

Smoke from the fire filled the air. Some of the chanters were obviously relatives and wailed more than chanted. Then came the moment when the curandero (healer) approached the fire with a large bowl, removed ashes from the fire and mixed them in with the concoction in the bowl. It occurred to Andrea that these were ashes from the body of Chucon. The curandero then approached Tinto, the chief, and handed him the bowl. Tinto drank a sip and then handed the bowl back to the curandero. This was repeated with the person standing next to Tinto, and so on.

Andrea looked at Brandon and asked, "Is that what I think it is?"

"Yes," he said. "When it comes to you, just keep your lips pursed together."

Andrea was near panic. "Oh my God! Do I have to accept the bowl?"

"It would be a severe insult if you did not," Brandon whispered. "Just play along so we can get the hell out of here!"

Eventually, the bowl did come to their side of the fire. Brandon took the bowl before Andrea and she watched carefully to see what he did. Then the curandero handed her the bowl. She took a very deep breath, closed her eyes and placed the bowl to her lips, turned it up and pretended she was swallowing. She wasn't sure whether she had been convincing or not, but it was very dark and that probably helped, she thought. She handed the bowl back to the curandero who seemed to be satisfied.

The ring around the fire seemed to break apart after the last person had sipped from the bowl.

Brandon made their apologies and the entire entourage climbed into Jeeps for the ride back to the Jungle Inn. Halfway there, Andrea asked Brandon to stop. She jumped out of the Jeep just in time, bent over and vomited.

Brandon got out, came around and held her head for her as she purged. Soon, she was empty and weak, but got back into her seat and was ready to continue. She wanted a long, hot shower, and then sleep to try and put some of this day behind her.

CHAPTER TEN

"Lost City of the Monkey God"

ANDREA TOSSED AND TURNED UNTIL THE WEE HOURS. HER mind just wouldn't rest, and somehow, the sounds of the tree frogs outside the window seemed louder than usual. Finally, when she did doze, it was more like passing out and she did not wake until the sun was up.

Brandon was not in the room. She rose and dressed, then went looking for him. She found him, Didier and Antonio gathered at a table in the bar/restaurant, engaged in deep conversation. As she approached, Didier was the first to spot her and rose from his chair, followed by the two other men. Brandon helped her with her chair, the waiter brought her a steaming cup of dark coffee. Nodding thanks, she turned to the men at the table. "Good morning!"

"Good morning," they all replied in unison. "I hope I wasn't disturbing anything?" she asked more than said.

"No, not at all," Didier replied. "We were just discussing The Lost City of the Monkey God."

"Ah!" Andrea said, blowing on her coffee to cool it. "Are we going there today?"

"Yep," Brandon replied. "The chopper will be here in about thirty minutes."

"Chopper?"

"It's the only way to get in there. The jungle is way too dense for any vehicle, or even mules for that matter," Antonio commented.

Didier spoke up. "Would you by any chance have room for one more on that helicopter?"

Antonio nodded. "I'd be proud to have you join us."

Breakfast was brought out. Scrambled eggs and bacon made from wild boar. Fried plantains and plenty of fresh fruit. Everyone ate their fill and went back to their respective rooms to gather things. In Andrea's case, it was plenty of bug spray and her camera, with several rolls of film.

She was walking out of the room when she heard the faint sounds of a helicopter approaching. She went directly to the landing in front of the hotel, just as the chopper was setting down in the parking lot.

It was a tight fit, between the trees and the building. She hoped the accuracy of the pilot was no accident.

As she was helped on board, Andrea was somewhat comforted to see that the aircraft was a modern (EC-130) ECO-Star, one of the most comfortable helicopters built. She had been worried that here in the jungle, she would be trapped into riding on some rickety old air buggy held together with baling wire, chewing gum and duct tape. She buckled herself into the plush leather seat and prepared herself, physically and emotionally for the lift-off.

Brandon, Naja, Antonio and Didier now climbed on board, chatting comfortably and commenting on the modern aircraft. Once they were buckled in, the pilot increased the RPMs and they lifted off.

Once in the air, Andrea looked down at the vast green jungle canopy. Her mind was racing with more than one thought. For openers, although she was enjoying the ride on this modern aircraft, she couldn't help but wonder what kind of money was behind this exploration and from who. Archaeologists are notoriously underfunded, existing on grants from universities. And this dig was apparently generated here in Central America. Or was it?

Where was she going, and why was Brandon's presence so important to Antonio? What was The Lost City of the Monkey God? Antonio's words echoed in her head; 'Many secrets are hidden within the darkness of the jungle.' What secret could be potentially fifteen hundred years old? She looked over at Brandon. He seemed as nonchalant as ever, looking out the window of the chopper. She didn't know why, but a shiver suddenly went through her.

The pilot announced they would be landing within five minutes. Then, Andrea started seeing signs of excavation, places where the jungle was being cleared, and remnants of stone buildings including pyramids.

The ancient Mayan archaeological site was massive. There must have been more than one hundred thousand people here in ancient times, she thought. She saw pyramids, government buildings, courtyards, ballcourts where games were played that ended in death.

Suddenly the chopper began to descend. Andrea wondered once again what she had gotten herself into. Normally, she would breathe a sigh of relief when she felt a chopper sit down. This time, she wasn't sure what to feel. She wasn't in any rush to get off the helicopter, that was for sure.

The pilot shut the chopper down completely. He was obviously going to wait for the party of four plus one jaguar. He would probably perform basic maintenance and point checks and refueling while he waited. Andrea couldn't help but notice the large fuel tank adjacent to the landing pad. She wondered how they had gotten it here, but there was little time to wonder, because barely had the blades on the machine stopped turning than she was greeted by a wild, white fronted capuchin monkey that came right up to her as if it had never seen a human before. It sat at her feet, looked up at her and chattered, as if it were asking who she was and what she was doing here.

The men in the group saw what was happening and laughed. Andrea wanted to reach down and pet the little animal, but it was wild, and she had no doubt she would be bitten. Then the monkey ran to Brandon and without hesitation, jumped up and grabbed the hem of his shorts to climb its way into his arms as if for protection.

Oddly, no one in the little party seemed to think anything was strange about this; not Antonio, not Didier, and when she thought about it, not her. Strangest of all, the monkey had ignored its natural enemy, the jaguar, in order to bravely approach the tall man who now embraced it.

The fact that the forest creature had approached her so completely without fear was an indication of just how remote this place was, and evidence that no human beings had been here in modern times. Amazing, she thought. She wouldn't have believed there was any place like this left on earth.

Antonio began something of a tour without delay or ceremony. Most of the things she saw at first were pretty much the same as she had seen when visiting other Mayan cities as a tourist. Archaeologists had set up something of a tent city not far from the landing pad and turned it into a camp. Many of their discoveries were brought here, waiting to be transported out. The tents also served as cover for some of their scientific equipment.

Andrea was busy with her camera, snapping photos of amazing things such as the inscriptions carved into walls and the huge stela positioned before pyramids that told of the personage honored there and their history. She had never been to such a 'new' site before. That is to say, one that was recently discovered and for the most part, pristine and unexcavated.

Antonio droned on for at least an hour until he approached a stone carving lying on the ground, about the size of a basketball. There, he stopped. Without a word, Brandon squatted down to inspect the carving. "What is it?" he asked.

"You've obviously heard of a were-wolf," Antonio said cautiously. "This is a were-jaguar. There are dozens of these things all over the site, from one end to the other."

"What do they mean?" Brandon asked.

Antonio shook his head back and forth. "Something was here."

"What do you mean, 'something was here'? What was it and how do you know?" Brandon asked, for some reason a little irritated.

"The Maya dreamed up all sorts of crazy stuff. Gods for everything. Gods of Rain, Gods of the Corn... Monkeys were depicted as the scribes. Essentially, the Maya were full of shit."

"Something was here," Antonio repeated.

"You already said that. But you haven't said *how* you know." Brandon repeated.

"That comes next," Antonio said. Then he started walking toward a large, elaborately platformed pyramid that had a large stela in front of it and an opening excavated into the base on one side. "Come with me," he motioned.

Andrea looked at Brandon. She sensed a foreboding unlike anything she had ever felt before in her life. Didier had been strangely quiet since the chopper landed, taking everything in as if he were absorbing every detail. The little group followed Antonio toward the pyramid. Naja remained tight against Brandon's side.

First, they paused at the stela. Andrea hadn't paid that much attention to it before now, but on closer inspection, she saw that it too was carved into the shape of the 'were-jaguar' as

Antonio had described it. She snapped photos of the stela from every possible angle. At first it was a curiosity. But then it occurred to her, configured the way it was in front of this pyramid, that moved the image out of the pantheon of supernatural Gods worshipped by the Maya, and made a declaration that this was a real being. It's the only way there could be a stela carved in his honor.

The group made their way inside the pyramid via the hole that had been dug into the side. Antonio flipped a switch that turned on battery powered lights which had been set up inside the pyramid. There was a chamber as big as a large dining room, and right in the middle of it, there was a sarcophagus, opened. Inside that sarcophagus was a skeleton; but this was no ordinary skeleton.

Most Maya were around four feet tall. This skeleton had belonged to a person at least six feet tall. He would have been a giant by Mayan standards. But that wasn't the frightening part. As Andrea snapped pictures and looked closer at the personage, her attention was drawn to the skeletons hands which were not hands at all, but large paws, complete with claws.

She slowly lowered the camera, staring at the skeleton. For some reason, she had a flashback to her first day in Honduras when she had heard two roars erupt from inside the Temple of the Black Jaguar.

She felt weak, as if she couldn't breathe. She had to get out of this dark, confined area. She turned and staggered for the opening to the outside. She heard Brandon's voice behind her say, "Are you alright?"

She didn't answer. She just needed to get outside and away from that…thing, whatever it was. Suddenly Brandon there at her side, helping to support her. She made it as far as the round altar stone placed before the stela, but she needed to sit and get control of herself.

"What's the matter? What's happening?" she heard Brandon saying.

"Just too much," she gasped. "Too much heat, too much drama with the snakes. Now this, a story straight out of Bram Stoker's Dracula. I need time to process."

Brandon looked at her as if he were confused by her words. "Help me back to the helicopter," she said. "I'll wait for you there. We are planning on going back today, aren't we? I mean, we're not going to spend the night here?"

"We're going back," Brandon assured her. After resting for a couple of minutes, Andrea stood up and started walking back toward the helicopter pad, although she staggered more than walked. She didn't want to spend another second close to this pyramid. "Cursed" was the only word she could think of to describe what she had just seen.

"Many secrets are hidden within the darkness of the jungle," Antonio had said. Those words kept hitting replay over and over in Andrea's head as the helicopter floated over the vast, green jungle canopy. He hadn't been bluffing. "Many secrets are hidden within the darkness of the jungle." He should have added, "Some of them will scare the shit out of you."

Only Brandon, Naja and Didier were on this return flight with her. Antonio stayed behind, at The Lost City of the Monkey God, to resume his work. There had been some kind of intense conversation between Brandon and Antonio which Didier was witness to, before Brandon climbed on the helicopter. Andrea had been sitting in the helicopter and been able to understand what they had said. But at one point, Brandon got heated and looked like he was reading Antonio the riot act.

Andrea's thoughts were interrupted when Brandon touched her on the shoulder and said, "What's bugging you?"

Andrea smiled a wry smile. "Well, Brandon, it's been a

rather eventful couple of days. This time yesterday, a man who worked for us was killed. A very young man, a kid, whose life was still ahead of him. We were expected to become cannibals in order to show respect for him. Today I am led into a fifteen-hundred-year-old lost city in the jungle and shown a skeleton, which is proof positive, of a... a... mutant being of some kind that may have been part jaguar. Excuse me but I'm trying my best to not hit emotional overload here." Tears flowed from Andrea as she looked at Brandon. She was shaking involuntarily.

Brandon looked surprised. "Don't tell me you believe that bullshit with the skeleton," he said.

"What am I supposed to believe? I saw it. It's there. It's evidence. It's real, for God's sake."

"Not necessarily. Look, a long time ago, in antiquity, some followers of a jaguar cult or something put that stupid skeleton together using pieces of a human and pieces of a jaguar skeleton to support their bullshit beliefs. You've seen the exact same thing in modern times. They do that same kind of crap in carnivals all the time. These were just some ancient con men that did it a long time ago. That's all. Look, there's a book you need to read sometime called the *Popul Vuh*. It's the Maya version of a Bible, written by the Quiche' Maya in Guatemala. Read it and you'll understand just how full of shit those people were."

Andrea thought about Brandon's words for a minute. "Okay, what about the size? This guy was two feet taller than an average Maya."

"Same song, different verse. They pieced together bones from lord knows what. I'm sure when scientists get hold of that stupid thing in a lab, they'll find all sorts of bones have been substituted."

"You really think so?"

"Absolutely! I know so without a doubt. When you read the

Popol Vuh, you'll read about a couple of characters called The Hero Twins. These assholes got killed and grew back as pumpkins. Now, the thing about it is, the Quiche' Maya didn't try to pass this stuff off as fantasy, a day with Christopher Robin in the Hundred Acre Wood. They sold it as fact. So, if you're willing to believe that bullshit, then maybe it's time we gave credence to a 'were jaguar'. Whaddaya think?"

Andrea thought it over. Brandon's explanation made sense. And certainly, they must have had jokers in Mayan times just as today. There was, for example, evidence that a type of counterfeiting was done with chocolate beans by removing the chocolate inside a chocolate bean husk and substituting it with mud. Yeah, she decided. She was driving herself nuts over nothing.

But then she thought, what about that stela in front of the ornately decorated pyramid? The one with the man's body and the jaguar's head and claws for hands? And what about all those goddamned stone effigies laying all over the place that the archaeologists had dubbed 'were-jaguars'? Was an entire ancient city in on the joke? A city of perhaps one hundred thousand people or more? Was a cult in charge of the city that believed in such an outrageous being?

Before she knew it, the helicopter was descending into the parking lot of the Jungle Inn. She sighed with relief.

Somehow this place seemed safe compared to The Lost City of the Monkey God. She was glad to be at her home away from home.

The aircraft had barely sat down before she was unbuckling her seat belt and out the door, moving like a rabbit toward her and Brandon's room. All she could think of was a long, hot shower.

Later that evening, in the bar, she allowed Didier's magic jungle juice to relax her and take her away from what she had seen and the myriad of questions that kept swirling around in her head. The more she had tried not to think about it, the more she thought about it. She let the rum take her away.

During their absence, Lorenzo had managed to get things together and departed for Jungle Cargo. He was probably there by now, she thought. Oh God! They would be unboxing all those snakes, putting them in the pit. She hoped they did so safely, with no more accidents.

She was pleasantly surprised to see Didier approach her table.

"May I sit?" he politely asked.

"By all means," Andrea responded.

"I have a little gift for you," Didier said with a smile. He handed her a gorgeous piece of jade, made into a pendant, slung with a narrow leather lanyard. Andrea held the stone and looked at it closely. It was handmade. A miniature carving of her face, and Brandon's, looking at one another; but above them was the highly detailed carving of a jaguar's head. "This is exquisite," she said. "You did this?"

Didier proudly nodded yes. "It's a little hobby of mine. I call this piece, 'Two Faces of The Jaguar'."

"Two Faces of The Jaguar," Andrea repeated. "Thank you, Didier." Andrea tied the ends of the leather lanyard in a square knot and slipped it over her neck. "Seems like everybody around here is trying to tell me something without telling me something!" she thought to herself. How many more surprises awaited her? This safari into the Mosquitia had been a cornucopia of surprises. She felt like she was about to hit overload.

CHAPTER ELEVEN

"Secrets Revealed"

THE TRIP OUT OF THE MOSQUITIA HAD BEEN A DIFFICULT ONE.
Rains had made the usually bad road even worse.

Although the Jeep was four-wheel drive, they had managed
to get stuck in some deep truck ruts and had to recruit a half
dozen Hondurans to help push them out.

Andrea removed herself from the misery by thinking back
to their fond farewell of Didier. The thought made her smile.
She loved Didier. Not in 'that' way, but like a dear friend, a
brother. He was certainly somebody she admired tremendously.
Here was a man who had overcome all the challenges that life
hurled against him and emerged not only triumphant but
made himself into a gentleman as well. Amazing! And as far as
Andrea was concerned, it was a good life lesson. She would
remember Didier, and his precious hand-made gift to her,
always.

By the time they finally reached Jungle Cargo, Andrea was
beyond exhausted and fed up with this whole damn scene. She
had not managed to accomplish one goal she had set for
herself before coming to this place. Well, maybe one. But she

was too bushed to worry about that one way or the other at the moment. What she needed for the next twenty-four hours was rest. She bathed, kissed Brandon goodnight, although it was late afternoon, and went to bed. Her head had barely hit the pillow before she was out like a light.

Somewhere in her dreams, she thought she heard a voice that she recognized, although not one she particularly liked; the voice of Felipe Quintanilla, the obnoxious 'doctor' customer who purchased all of Brandon's snakes and had a standing order for more. In her dream, she got out of bed, staggered to the window and saw the man, out in the compound talking to Brandon. In her dream, Quintanilla handed Brandon a large box which Brandon quickly put in the tool shed. Then Quintanilla and Brandon had a loud discussion in which she heard

Brandon saying words like, "Last fucking time, *ever*!"

After a few minutes of not so friendly discussion, Quintanilla handed Brandon a fat envelope and left.

None of it made any sense. Quintanilla wasn't even in this country. What the hell, she thought. Dreams never made any sense anyway. Just like the one of Brandon in the garden surrounded by jaguars. She opened her eyes and found that she was in bed. Then she closed her eyes and for the next several hours, blackness took her.

When Andrea finally slowly surfaced back into consciousness, she found that it was daylight. She just wasn't sure it was the same day. She struggled to get out of bed and after making a brief stop in the potty, she walked to the window to peek out and see what she could see. She noticed that the house was strangely quiet and wondered where the girls were. Then she noticed there was no racket of any kind coming from the compound and wondered where all the men were. What she saw was Naja in her run, and that too was unusual because the big cat was normally at her master's side, like a lap dog.

From the corner of her eye, she noticed movement way out in the back of the compound, by the snake pit. Squinting, she saw that it was Brandon, doing something. She glanced around the room and didn't spot her binoculars, but there was a 300mm telephoto lens in her camera case which she quickly attached to her old Nikon and pulled focus on the action by the snake pit. What she saw was confusing and bizarre, and her right index finger went to the trigger as she began taking pictures.

Brandon was performing some kind of a weird operation in several parts. First, he would reach into the snake pit and withdraw a large fer-de-lance, then carefully lower the snake into a large, Igloo style cooler. He had several of the coolers lined up side by side.

When the snake was inside, he slammed the lid of that cooler, and repeated the action with the next cooler. She had to assume that he had ice in the coolers. For some reason, he was forcing the snakes into artificial hibernation, effectively knocking them out. But why? Her answer came in the next few minutes, and it made her stomach do flip flops.

After a snake had been in the cooler for about fifteen minutes, Brandon prepared a hypodermic needle with some kind of serum, then opened a cooler lid, gave the snake an injection about half way down its length, then withdrew the snake from the cooler while it was still in Lala land, forced its mouth open and, using small tongs, picked up what looked to be something the size of a pint sized sealed plastic bag which was slick with oil and manipulated it down the snake's gullet. Andrea got pictures of it all. But at the same time, she wanted to scream. Her heart was breaking. Tears filled her eyes and made it almost impossible to see, much less focus on the photos she was taking. She muttered curses under her breath as she clicked the shutter and advanced the film for the next shot.

She knew those plastic bags were filled with opium. Her real bosses had been right all along. Brandon Shaw was involved in the drug business. Not only that, he was the main pipeline, getting the most dangerous drug of all past the drug sniffing dogs at the Miami airport by cloaking the smell with the musk of snakes. Here was the evidence she had come for.

She continued watching, photographing. When Brandon had stuffed the snakes, she now realized the injections he was administering were some kind of drug to relax the snake's digestive system and prevent them from regurgitating the bags.

He would slip the loaded snake into a cloth snake bag and place that into a shipping box. When a box had been filled with three or four snakes, he would seal the crate with a wooden lid and nail it in place. Then the process would repeat.

Now she understood why he was always in the market for more snakes. She understood the hurried safari into the Mosquitia Jungle and the frenzy to capture as many snakes as possible.

She had to disentangle; divorce herself from her feelings for Brandon Shaw and do her job. Up until this point, he had been her hero. She loved him and doted on him. Not even Reggie's evidence had shaken her faith in him because there was no direct connection, no proof.

But now... God! Now she had to pull back, somehow, in order to do what she was sent here to do. That would not be easy. She had slipped and allowed herself to do something that had never happened before in her life; she had fallen in love, deeply in love, with a man who was supposed to be the target of an investigation. Her knees felt weak. She felt she could not stand any longer, and she sank down into a squatting position beside the window. Then, more tears came. She sobbed from a deep aching. She thought her heart would break.

It was sometime later that Brandon put away his things and started walking toward the house. By then, Andrea had taken at least a hundred photos of his activities. She carefully put the camera and film away and climbed back into bed, pretending she was still asleep.

A minute later, she heard the front door open. Brandon came tromping through the house. She heard him stop at the bedroom door. Then he turned and walked away, into the kitchen.

It was time to get up, but just then she heard the old blue truck arriving from wherever Lorenzo had been with it. The girls had been with him. They apparently went into town for groceries, and Lorenzo had gone to the lumber yard for materials to build shipping crates. A big shipment was imminent. Doug would be arriving from Florida. Andrea had work to do. She hopped out of bed.

After hastily dressing, she went down the stairs and made her way out into the compound where Brandon was busy helping Lorenzo unload wood from the truck. "Hi!" she said, trying to sound as cheerful as possible.

Brandon stopped what he was doing. "Hi!" he replied.

"Must be getting ready for a shipment," she said.

"Yeah," Brandon said, sounding bored. "Same old crap all over again."

"Wow! That doesn't sound like enthusiasm," Andrea quipped.

Brandon looked away and smiled a wry smile. "Enthusiasm? There's something I haven't felt in a long time."

Andrea had an idea that had been brewing in her head for quite some time. Her mother had taught her to never just throw the baby out with the bath water, that people always gave up on something too quickly.

Now, in this most confusing, crucial and dire moment, that

training might help her to prevent a breaking heart. But she would have to broach the next topic carefully.

"You know, I've sensed a tiredness in you ever since I've been here. If you aren't happy, why don't you close this place down? Animal protection laws are closing in on you anyway."

Brandon looked at Andrea. "And do what? This is all I know. What am I supposed to do for a living, shine shoes on the corner in downtown La Ceiba?"

Andrea shrugged. "You're an intelligent man. There's any number of things you should be able to do."

"Intelligent? Yeah, in my world I am intelligent. You see me in my natural environment. My 'habitat'. But can you imagine me in a frigging office, wearing a suit?"

"I'll bet you would look handsome in a suit."

"I would look like a fool, because that's what I would be. A two-hundred-pound monkey on the end of a string, not knowing what the fuck I was doing or why I was doing it."

"Why are you doing this?"

"Because it's the only goddamned thing I know how to do. Now let's talk about something else if you don't mind."

Andrea turned and started walking away. "I'll be back later. I'm going to town."

"Town?"

"I need some girl things."

"I thought you had some of those 'things'."

"Not 'those' things, some other girl things. Don't worry about it."

Brandon looked a little resigned but turned back to helping Lorenzo.

Andrea went upstairs, grabbed her purse, camera and tote bag, bounced back down the steps, jumped into the Jeep and took off down the trail toward the main road to town.

When she arrived at the main road and turned west, into town, she reached into her purse and withdrew her cell phone.

After dialing a two-digit code, she held the phone to her ear and waited. After a moment,

"Meet me at a restaurant called the Las Palmas in 45 minutes." After listening for a minute, she hung the phone up and tossed it back in her purse.

Close to an hour later, she pulled up in front of the Las Palmas Restaurant and parked, collected her purse and tote bag and hurried in the front door. Inside, it was dark compared to the bright sun, so she had a little trouble adjusting to the light. At last, she spotted the person she had come here to see. His name was David Harkness, and he was a special agent for the DEA. He was also Andrea's supervisor. David was deceptive in his appearance. He looked like anything but a fed. True, he was the right size, medium build, six feet tall, angular with sandy brown hair, in his fifties. But the expression on his face was friendly, not threatening, and he wore a popular Central American shirt called a guayavera. Despite the heat, he wore long trousers, which also helped him blend in with the Central American milieu. When he saw Andrea approaching, he rose to shake hands with her.

"David."

"Andrea. I'm guessing this meeting means you've made a breakthrough."

"Yes, I have. But we need to have a talk. There's some rather unique circumstances involved."

"Unique circumstances?" David Harkness looked at Andrea suspiciously. "That doesn't sound like you. You're not a 'unique circumstances' kind of woman."

"I've come up against some things in this case unlike anything we've ever encountered before."

"Like what?"

"It's too complicated to explain here, and believe me, it would take too long. Look, I've got the goods on Shaw, but the plain truth is, this guy is as much a victim as he is a perp in this whole damn kettle of fish."

"How can he be a victim?" David said. "He's a drug dealer. Drug dealers are not victims."

———

Andrea looked down at the table for a moment. Just then the waiter arrived with menus. After ordering drinks, the waiter retreated. "I want you to work with me on this, David. I've never asked for a goddamn thing before, ever. Not since I've been with the agency. Look, I know who's on the receiving end, the distributor of the drugs. I know how he's getting them. Shaw may actually be getting blackmailed into this shit. The distributor, he's the real bad guy in all this. I think the same guy is even involved in the manufacture. Let's bring it down around the ears of the real bad guys and leave Shaw out of the net."

"You must have slipped a cog."

"Shaw is only involved in transportation. He is not involved in manufacturing. He is not involved in the distribution. If we cut off the supply, his part will dry up. Look, Brandon Shaw got caught up in this because he's running scared. The animal business is going to hell. He doesn't know any other way to make a living. This is all he's done his whole life. Now that the faucet is slowly being turned off where animals are concerned, he's hit the panic button. He's frightened of losing everything and starving. That's all."

"That's not our problem," David Harkness said.

"Yeah, it is our problem," Andrea said, looking at David in a pleading way.

David stared at Andrea, searching what was in her eyes. "What's going on here? Have you gone and gotten emotionally involved with this bozo?"

Andrea looked down at the tablecloth. "He's not 'just' a

bozo. He's a most remarkable bozo. He has a good heart. I think I can rehabilitate him if I have the chance."

"Oh shit! You *have* gotten emotionally involved. Sonofabitch! Have you slept with him too?"

"That's not important."

"The hell it's not. You must be crazy!" David said sharply. "He's a criminal. You can't rehabilitate a criminal. You're gonna mess around and fuck up your whole career, and it's been a good one for you so far."

"It hasn't been all that great!" Andrea confessed.

David was quiet for several moments. "So, what you saying is, you're willing to throw it all away, and roll the dice on a known criminal because you think you can turn him around? Or maybe just because he's good in the sack?"

Andrea nodded her head. "Yeah, I guess that's what I'm saying."

David looked at Andrea long and hard. "Fuck me!" He muttered under his breath. "You know, they always warned me about things like this happening when you work with a woman. But I thought you were different. Actually, you have been…up until now."

Andrea looked at David pleadingly. "I've worked for you almost twenty years. How many times have I asked for a favor?"

"Never. This job isn't about favors. This isn't like selling cars at Honest Bob's. This is about stopping criminals from polluting our society. There's just no flexibility, no room for stuff like 'favors'."

"The hell you say! This time it is. Remember what you said to me when I brought it down around the ears of Ochoa in six months and the bureau thought it would take at least two years?"

"That was just an expression of gratitude."

"Well, not to me it wasn't, you sonofabitch. You didn't

make it sound that way at the time. Not to me. I'm calling you on that favor, David. If you welch on me now, I'll walk, and I'll take my evidence with me."

David thought about it for a long moment, sighed a deep sigh. "What have you got for me?"

"Have we got a deal?" she pressed.

"Against my better judgement…yeah, a deal. I don't want to lose you. You've been too good an agent. But I want you to know I consider this out and out blackmail."

"You can consider it a chicken pot pie if you want to."

David Harkness smiled, although he didn't want to. "What have you got for me?" he repeated.

Andrea reached in her tote bag and withdrew a tall kitchen sized, plastic, draw string garbage sack filled with rolls of film and placed it on the table. "I've got everything for you. There are pictures of a poppy field where they're growing some of the stuff, practically right under our noses. Pictures of the lab where they're processing."

"But we still don't know how they're getting it in," David said.

"Yeah, we do!" Andrea said with resignation and sadness in her voice.

"We do?" David's attention peaked.

"Brandon Shaw is stuffing bags of smack down the gullets of some very poisonous, very dangerous snakes. Those snakes are part of every shipment to Florida. There's a customer there waiting to buy every snake that comes in. He has a standing order."

"Quintanilla?"

"Felipe Quintanilla. He's the kingpin behind this entire magilla. Put him out of business and Shaw's part instantly dries up."

"What about Shaw's partner?"

"Doug? Poor Doug. All this stuff is going on around him

and he doesn't have a clue. But the thing that can stop it on that end without having to send anybody to prison is enforcing encroachment laws. Prohibit export of as many animals as possible from Honduras. Enact protected species lists on the American side. Have the federal fish and game boys take a meeting with Doug Bennet and let him know what's coming. Just, leave Shaw out of it. He's completely off limits. Everything dries up around him, he's got to get out and do something else for a living."

"What's going on with you and this Shaw guy? I want the truth, Andrea."

Andrea looked away. "It's complicated. I just…"

"Love is always complicated," David said.

His comment surprised Andrea. She smiled. "Why David, you're an old softie in disguise!"

"Shhhh. Goddamn. Don't tell anybody! I've got a reputation…"

"Your secret is safe with me," Andrea said with a giggle.

At that moment, an inebriated, obese man staggered past where Andrea and David were sitting and bumped hard against their table, knocking the plastic garbage bag off the table, onto the floor. He apologized, picked up the bag and replaced it on the table, then staggered on.

Andrea grabbed quickly for the bag. She looked around on the floor and thought all its contents were intact, but not so. Two rolls of her precious, exposed film rolled out through the loose, untied top and far under the table. From her perspective, Andrea did not see the rolls, but someone else did. Sitting at a table some twenty feet away, being very quiet so as not to be noticed was Marta Saldana.

She saw, and she waited. She also listened. But because there was relaxing music playing at a low volume over the restaurant's PA system, she couldn't make out the conversation going on between Andrea and the man whom Marta Saldana did not recognize. All she knew was, this looked suspicious and she would use it to her best advantage.

Eventually, the meeting between Andrea and David came to an end. David paid the bill, retrieved the trash bag filled with rolls of film and he and Andrea left together. The minute they were gone, Marta went over to their vacated table and tried to rake the film toward her with her foot. When that didn't work, she told the waiter she had dropped the rolls and asked if he would retrieve them from under the table for her. He politely did so.

Now she had it! She had a weapon to use against that blonde bitch who had stolen her Brandon away from her. Oh, this was a grand day! A blessed day! A day better than anything she could have ever hoped for.

There was no doubt the meeting between her and the stranger was something bad for Brandon. She would rescue her man and get him back in one fell swoop and send the blonde chinga to hell in the process.

Marta Saldana was smiling and chuckling to herself as she left the Las Palmas, clutching her rolls of film.

Andrea had done it, she thought as she drove the Jeep to the nearest pharmacia to buy something, anything that would make it look like a trip to town was justified.

She had pulled it off. She would be able to bring down the bastard that was behind all of this without destroying the man she loved, whom she saw as a prisoner of his own making. She thanked her mother for the sage advice, "Never throw the baby out with the bath water." "Thanks, Mom!" Andrea said to the air.

She had told David about the mega shipment of snakes that would be coming to the United States in a few days and set things up for Quintanilla to get busted as soon as he had the shipment in his "lab." But that is where the trail would end. Quintanilla would disappear into the system. Andrea would then have a chance to rehabilitate Brandon. With luck, everything would work out like clockwork, just the way she had planned. True, there were more than a few 'ifs' to her plan, but all of them were worth it if there was any chance at all that she could pull Brandon out of the fire. His life was worth saving. As little as she knew about him so far, she knew that much to be true. She was willing to bet on it and at this point, she had! She had put her career on the line. Be that as it may, she felt like a truck had been lifted off her.

The following morning, Jungle Cargo was in full swing. Lorenzo and Pablo were furiously building shipping crates and making all preparations for a shipment. Doug had been contacted and was due to arrive the next morning. Everything looked so 'normal'. Busy as hell, but normal.

By late afternoon, the big blue truck was loaded and ready for the trip to the airport the next morning. Activity slowed, and Brandon told everyone to go home for a good night's rest. This left him and Andrea alone. She took advantage of the evening to prepare a romantic supper on the veranda, complete with candlelight and wine.

There were advantages to living forty feet from the Caribbean. Fishermen were constantly passing by in their cayucos selling their catch which ranged anywhere from fresh snook to spiny lobster, which were plentiful this time of year. Andrea managed to make a deal on a couple of three pounders. Her meal would consist of lobster, hearts of palm salad and baked plantains.

The evening was textbook. Everything was perfect, the meal, the small conversation, the bright moon overhead. And then, after the bottle of wine was finished, she led Brandon into the bedroom where she melted into his arms and for a few hours, the world was very far away

A cocoon surrounded them as they enriched their relationship with deep, tender passion. She gave herself to him completely. Not just physically, but spiritually. She thought of Didier's gift to her, the pendant which he called *Two Faces of the Jaguar.* Surely, in soul, she and this man she held so tightly were one.

This was all so new to her, she thought. All her life, she had been focused on one thing. Even in college, she knew exactly what she wanted to do with her future. She wanted to be a DEA agent. Heroin had taken her father in Viet Nam, and although that was a country a world away, she grew up painfully aware of the prevalence of the problem in her own country. To be an enemy of it was all she had ever thought about, and she had dedicated her life to that prospect. She had never even considered falling in love.

This had blind-sided her. She was in uncharted territory. She knew it was dangerous, but she was drawn to this man as inexorably as a moth to a flame. She would have to handle whatever danger came with it as it presented itself. She knew now that she had no choice. No choice but to hold on tight and go for the ride.

At the airport the following morning, Doug gave Andrea a big hug and a knowing smile. "You sure you don't want to hop on here and come back to Florida?" he chided.

"I'm sure. There's a lot to do here. Besides, looks to me like the last thing you need is another pound on this airplane."

"Yeah, you could be right," Doug said, looking into the cargo hold. "Haven't seen these many snakes in years. I'm glad I won't have to do anything except hand the boxes over to our client in Miami. We don't have room to store half this many reptiles."

"I know. Okay, have a safe flight."

Doug gave her another hug, then shook hands with Brandon and Lorenzo. With a smile, Doug got on the plane, slammed the door and a minute later could be seen strapping himself into the pilot's seat.

As Brandon, Andrea and Lorenzo stepped away from the plane, Doug revved the engines and turned toward the taxiway.

As Doug took off, Andrea secretly crossed her fingers that everything would go as planned in Florida. The trap was set. With luck, by nightfall, Quintanilla would be looking out at the world through bars.

CHAPTER TWELVE

End of an Era

THINGS RETURNED TO NORMAL AT JUNGLE CARGO. THE NEXT morning rose clear and calm. The girls prepared the standard fruit fest and set everything up out on the front deck. Everyone gathered for the morning 'desayuno' and unofficial meeting to roughly sketch out the day.

Andrea was pleased to see that everyone seemed relaxed. There was a lot of joking and laughing. Lorenzo had let Naja out of her run, and she joined them, sitting faithfully at Brandon's side and nudging him with her head more like a golden retriever than a jaguar. Andrea never ceased to be amazed by the animal. She was beautiful, deadly, tame as a pussycat and loyal as a dog. Who would have believed it?

Eventually, the gathering broke up and everyone went their respective ways to do whatever they had to do. Andrea discovered that the day following a shipment was slightly altered from standard days. There were far fewer animals in the cages that needed tending, so, the girls were able to turn their focus to the house. For instance, scrubbing and polishing Brandon's wood floors that he was so proud of.

Pablo Palma did maintenance duties around the

compound. Lorenzo needed to run into town for a myriad of errands. And Brandon, well, Brandon did an inspection of everything. But mostly, he seemed a little lost, like a kid that had misplaced his favorite toy. He also looked worried. He walked out to the beach and stared at the horizon. Andrea watched him for a few minutes, then decided to join him.

"What's on your mind, Bwana?" she asked as she approached.

"Don't know," he said as he shook his head. "Something… maybe a lot of things. I'm sick to death of this business. But I'm as trapped as one of those monkeys in a cage back there. I don't know a fucking thing else. I want out. I'm tired of taking animals out of the jungle. I'm tired of the jungle. I'm sick and tired of the whole thing." He stooped down and picked up a sand dollar, then frizbeed it out, toward the water.

"You ever thought about working as a consultant in a zoo, something like that?"

"Consultant? I don't have any degrees. All my knowledge comes from buying them or catching them and selling them. That hardly qualifies me as a zoologist."

"Tell me, Brandon, what has that experience and knowledge taught you?"

Brandon paused for a moment, then he shocked Andrea with his answer. "It's taught me that it is absolutely wrong to remove these animals from the jungle."

Andrea was non-plussed.

"What? I don't disagree. As a matter of fact, I totally agree, but I'm shocked to hear *you* say it."

"Why? You think I'm blind, or without feelings for these creatures?"

"Why no, but," she indicated the compound with a sweep of her arm.

"I fell into this pile of shit when I was young and stupid. I was a rebel, didn't want to finish school. I grew up in Florida, had a good family. My dad was a geologist. Mom was a housewife. But I just didn't fit in. I always wanted to know what was just over the next hill. Ran away from home when I was fifteen. Started hitchhiking.

"Somehow, I wound up down here working for a real asshole. That was my first job in the animal business. Then I went to Peru, way up the Amazon River to Leticia. That was a rape scene if I ever saw one."

"What do you mean?"

"No animal protection laws at all. None! Exporters were paying Indians to bring them every creature known to man. They even had tropical fish farms set up. The damned Indians were seining the rivers and getting rich, at least by their standards."

"So…how did you wind up back here?"

"Got sick to my stomach from what I saw in Peru. Plus… something drew me here. I wanted to study the Maya Indians. But I needed to make a living, so I started Jungle Cargo.

"Since then, what can I tell you? I grew up! And being up close to it like this, I can see even more what it's doing. Each little animal, no matter how insignificant it may seem to us, has a specific job to do in that forest. If they aren't there to do it, the job doesn't get done. It manifests and sooner or later the jungle suffers. So does mankind, although we are too stupid to know what's causing the pain."

Andrea's mouth was agape. She had been totally caught off guard by this, had no idea Brandon felt the way he did.

"The only thing it doesn't bother me to ship out of here are the parrots," he said, as he flung another sand dollar into the surf.

"Why the parrots?" Andrea asked.

"Because, the fruit companies kill them by the thousands," Brandon said almost too casually.

"What!"

"Yep!" Another sand dollar went into the surf.

"Fruit companies don't just grow bananas down here. They also grow citrus, watermelons, cantaloupes, other stuff. A gang of parrots will fly into a field of watermelons and gnaw a hole about the size of a silver dollar into every damn watermelon. To keep that from happening, the fruit companies station men in the fields with shotguns. I've seen the backs of pickup trucks filled with dead, green bodies."

Andrea gasped. She had no idea. She was horrified.

Brandon scowled. "For a while, it was against the law to export them. I'm the one that made it possible," Brandon said.

"How?" Andrea asked.

"I spoke to the Honduran politicians in the language they understand best, graft! I went to Tegusigalpa and visited the boys at the department of recursos naturales, natural resources, and proposed that they issue me a papel cellado, a permit. The deal was, I would pay a specific tax on every bird I took out of here. In order to verify the number and species of birds, one of the politicos from Tegus would have to fly up here, at my expense of course, to do an inspection. Those 'inspection' trips always normally happen on weekends, so as not to interfere with regular work-days. Understand?"

"Oh, of course!"

"Inevitably, it involves booze, barbeque, whores and beach. It also involves paying 'the tax' which comes to about a hundred or so dollars more than what's listed on the papel cellado. If the inspector spends more than five minutes looking at the birds, somebody wins a bet. We time them, just for the fun of it!

"Anyway, with that paper, we can take a million birds out of here if we want. Doug quarantines them in Florida for two months, then we sell them to pet shops, zoos, what have you. At least they get to live instead of winding up in a green pile in the back of some rusty pickup truck. So, I don't feel guilty about extracting the birds. Just everything else."

"Even the snakes?"

Brandon looked down at the sand. "Especially the snakes. But that's another story."

"Another story?"

"Someday I'll tell you about it, maybe. But not today." Brandon tossed one last sand dollar into the surf, then brushed his hands off and turned to walk back to the house. His gait and body language reflected resignation. The man was tired. Soul sick and spirit tired.

"So now I know what Didier meant when he called this pendant 'Two Faces of The Jaguar'," Andrea said as she tried to catch up with Brandon. "I'm just not sure what he meant by the 'jaguar' part."

"Who knows," Brandon said. "He spends too much time in the middle of that stinking jungle. What else has he got to do besides dream stuff up? He needs a broad to distract him a little."

Andrea chuckled at that.

The small table in the carport beneath the house was Brandon's target. He landed in a chair with a sense of resignation.

It was now or never, time for Andrea to introduce her plan. Andrea seated herself next to him.

"You know, Brandon, all of that knowledge you have in that head of yours could not only make you a living but help animals in the process, *and* the jungle."

Brandon looked at Andrea, slightly confused. "What are you talking about?"

"I'm talking about touring. Touring and lecturing, telling about your years of experience in the jungle, what you've seen, what you've learned from first hand experience. Talking about what's happening down here."

"And just who would I regale with these captivating yarns?"

"Well, to begin with, zoo organizations, the directors, curators, the key personnel. They're a good starting place, but I have a feeling your popularity would spread like a brush fire."

"That's a Xanadu pipe dream."

"No. It's a very real possibility."

"Darling, I'm fixing to say something to you, and I say it with all the love in the world, no disrespect.

"Okay?"

"You're out of your fucking mind."

"No, Brandon. That kind of thing is very popular in the states right now. Besides, who do you think all these professors and learned people get their information from? People like you. *you* are their source."

"And how long do you think something like that would last before I burned out?"

"I don't see interest in what you have to say *ever* burning out. America is a big country. Besides, America isn't the only country. You speak Spanish. Lots of Spanish speaking countries have zoos. Barcelona has one of the biggest, for example. And personal appearances are just the beginning. I can see the possibility of a TV series."

Anna Maria appeared with a couple of cold beers and a dish of key limes, cut into quarters, and salt in the bottom of the dish. Brandon and Andrea thanked her, then continued their discussion.

Brandon took a deep drink of the cold beer. After thinking about what Andrea had said for a couple of minutes, he said, "If what you say is really possible, it might offer me a way out of here. I like the sound of it, but to be honest with you, it just sounds too good to be true."

"What if I send out some feelers. Take a poll, so to speak, and showed you the feasibility of it?"

Brandon looked at her for several moments without saying anything. Finally, "You're serious, aren't you?"

"Serious as a heart attack," Andrea countered. "Brandon, you don't have any idea what you're sitting on. You have knowledge that could make a huge difference, so huge that you could possibly be responsible for bringing about meaningful legislative change, not only about animal conservation, but saving the jungle. Tell you what, the very thing you are frightened of because you think it is your enemy may very well be your best friend."

"What do you mean?"

"These animal encroachment laws. Don't resent them, embrace them. From what you just told me, that's already the way you feel. Put it to good use."

Brandon looked away, thinking. Finally, he slowly nodded his head. "So, how would you send out 'feelers'?"

"With the computer. I have everything I need right there on the desk in your office."

Brandon sat quietly pondering the idea for several minutes. Finally, he said, "Okay. Send out some feelers. Let's see what happens."

Andrea smiled. "I'll start building a website tomorrow. This is the age of modern communication. I can do it all from right in your office or living-room with my computer and the internet."

She reached out and took Brandon's hand in hers. "Thank you, Brandon. I'm very excited. We can do it, Honey. I know we can."

They clinked beers and Andrea whooped. "Oh Lord! I can't believe it. This is a dream come true!"

Brandon agreed. "I can't believe it either. But let's chill and wait to see the results of a poll before we get too carried away."

Andrea started getting organized in her head. Anna Maria

brought more beers. She could sense the elation, even though she spoke no English.

"The first thing we need to do is register a name for a website. Then build the website. In this case we're going to need a lot of pictures, not only for the website, but also to use for your lectures. You know, visual aids, show and tell.

"I'll also help you, if you want me to. I'll design your presentation. I've done it before and I'm pretty good at it. It should last no more than forty-five minutes. Thirty minutes would be better. Oh, Brandon! This is so exciting!"

Brandon smiled. He was starting to imagine it and began seeing it in his mind. He had always considered Andrea a pretty amazing woman, he just had no idea how amazing until now. Like magic, she had created a path for him to get the hell out of the awful corner he had painted himself into. It was logical. He could see it working. He would do anything to get out of this stinking jungle and to 'not' do what the horrible pests in his life had talked him into doing because of his desperation.

"I'm going to need a different camera," he heard Andrea say.

"What?"

"The camera I have only shoots film. We need a digital camera, so we can take pictures and upload them onto the website, fast."

"Damn! When you get a bee in your bonnet, better get out of your way," Brandon said, laughing.

"I just don't think I've ever been this excited about anything," she said. "Brandon, I'm going to town, I need to look for a digital camera. You want to come with me?"

"Absolutely!" Brandon said.

Suddenly, his mood had done a 180. He was feeling good. The two lovers walked to the Jeep enthusiastically and took off for LaCeiba in a cloud of dust.

"We'll need lots of pictures of you in the jungle," Andrea said as they sped along.

"Doing what?" Brandon asked.

"Just doing what you do. That's the whole point. I already have a lot that I took in the Mosquitia; a lot of real good ones. But I'll have to get the film processed and then get a converter to change color slides into digital images."

"How are you going to do that in this God forsaken place?"

"I don't know. But I'll figure it out. Now that I know what I need to do, I'm not going to let details stop me, you can believe that."

"I *do* believe that," Brandon said, laughing.

In LaCeiba, the pair found a small camera shop which didn't have much to offer, but Andrea found a Canon that she liked. Brandon pulled a wad of cash out of his pocket to pay for it, then the two decided to stop and have lunch.

Following an hour of small talk and sumptuous seafood, they departed the restaurant, climbed into the Jeep and drove casually back to Jungle Cargo. Marta Saldana watched as the Jeep passed the post office, where she worked. Marta's eyes narrowed as she whispered under her breath, "Your day is coming, Chinga!"

Brandon was now emotionally committed to this transition and eventual departure which he preferred to call 'retirement.' He decided to have a front deck meeting with everybody the next morning and make the announcement.

When they got back to Jungle Cargo, Brandon called Doug in Florida to tell him. Doug listened as silent as death. "Well... this, this, this is quite a surprise,"

Doug stammered over the phone. "You say you're going to have a pow-wow with the troops tomorrow morning? Well, I should be there, uh, be there. I'll fly down this afternoon. Don't worry about coming to get me. I'll just grab a taxi. Grab a taxi."

"Are you sure?" Brandon asked.

"Yeah, it's easier. Just put fresh sheets on the bed in that spare room that it doesn't sound like Andrea is using anymore."

Brandon smiled. "Will do." He hung up the phone and turned to Andrea. "Doug is coming down."

"Wow!" she said, and what that translated to was, 'This is really happening.' She could hardly believe it. It all seemed too easy. It's true what they said about timing. Timing was everything.

The following morning was a little tense on the front deck. The girls set out the coffee pot and bowls of fresh fruit as usual, plus plenty of hard-boiled eggs. But you could see it in their eyes and their body language that they knew something was coming, and it probably wasn't good for them.

Doug had arrived safely and was standing by the front railing, coffee cup in hand. Brandon walked over to him, also with a coffee cup. "Did you sleep well?" Brandon asked.

"Strangely enough, like a baby," Doug said with a half-smile. He looked out at the flat Caribbean. "Never been able to get over how beautiful it is here, beautiful." Doug said.

"Deceptively so!" Brandon responded.

Lorenzo and Pablo now arrived and filled coffee cups, then bowls with fruit. They nodded and spoke a pleasant "Buenos Dias!" but you could tell, they knew something was in the wind and were apprehensive. Andrea came out of the house and said her good mornings, gave Doug a hug, then she put her arm around Brandon. Naja came up the stairs and went straight to her water dish before assuming her position beside Brandon's chair. The gang was all here.

"We might as well get started," Brandon said.

"In your hearts, you all knew this day was coming. You just didn't know when. But then, neither did I. Jungle Cargo is going to shut down operations within the next few months."

The girls, upon hearing those words immediately begin to cry. Lorenzo and Pablo looked stunned.

"For right now, we are going to continue to operate, but on a modified basis."

"What do you mean, modified?" Lorenzo asked.

"Modified means no more snakes, no more coati mundis, no more agoutis, no more prehensile tailed porcupines, no more monkeys, no more jaguarundis, no more cats of any kind, big or small. In short, we are not going to buy any kind of animals with the exception of parrots and other psittacine birds."

"No more snakes?" Pablo said, almost in shock.

"No more anything. Just birds. Pablo, you need to start breaking down everything except the flight cages. Fill in the snake pit with dirt. Don't touch Naja's run of course." Pablo stared at Brandon open mouthed and silent.

"Well, it might be for the best anyway...best anyway," Doug interjected. "I think our best reptile client might have gotten his tail in a twist of some kind."

"What do you mean?" Brandon said, slightly surprised.

"I dunno. I heard a rumor that he got cross ways with the feds, somehow. I tried to call, but nobody answers. I drove by his lab, it's closed. It's all very hush hush. Nobody seems to know anything. But if he isn't going to be, going to be buying snakes anymore, then we've got to cut back on snakes, or find another buyer. Let's face it, he was a key client. Key.

"But you know what? The timing is good anyway. A game and fish guy dropped by to check permits the other day and he told me that some new animal protection laws are coming down the pike that will definitely put us out in the cold. Animal protection laws, protected species lists, prohibited species lists. The timing is right. I mean, I mean, I don't like it, but from a practical standpoint, it's the right thing to do. If we keep doing what we're doing right now without looking down the road, we're gonna get caught with our pants down, sure as the world."

The meeting continued for another hour. Brandon detailed very carefully what would happen to Pablo, Lorenzo and the girls. They would all be cared for. So, they wouldn't walk away empty handed. But there was angst and sadness.

Jungle Cargo wasn't like a company. It was like a family, and these people felt they were losing their family. It helped that they would continue operations for at least three more months, but even that was too much finality, especially for the girls, who were inconsolable.

There were no animals to transport to Florida this soon after a shipment had been made. So, Doug hung around for a few more hours, then made his apologies and asked for a ride to the airport. Brandon and Andrea both escorted the company partner back to town.

"You seem relieved, uh, relieved," Doug commented as the Jeep made its way along the pothole filled road.

Brandon nodded acknowledgement. "I am," he said. "This has been coming for a long time, Doug. I haven't been happy, plus, I could see the handwriting on the wall. Anybody with the sense that God gave a tree frog could. It's inevitable. We're being legislated out of business. We're just doing something about it with the right timing for once."

"Good, good point," Doug agreed.

An hour later, Brandon and Andrea stood inside the terminal at the LaCeiba airport looking through the picture window at Doug taking off in the old company bomber.

"One day soon we'll be on that plane getting the hell out of here for good," Brandon said.

Then they turned away and walked toward the front of the terminal, out the door and to the Jeep.

On the way back through town, they spotted Doc coming

out the front door of the Mazapan Hospital. They honked and pulled over. "Where you going, Viejo?" Brandon asked.

"Lunch, then siesta," Doc replied.

"Well, good," Brandon said. "Why don't you jump in and let us buy you lunch. We have something important to tell you."

"Important news?" Doc said and hopped into the Jeep.

Thirty minutes later, Doc sat at a table across from Bandon and Andrea, looking at them as if he had just been given a shot of Novocain. He was speechless. It was obvious he wanted to say something. Instead, all he could do was toss his martini back and order another one by pointing to his glass.

Finally, "You know, I'm a doctor. All I do is work. I don't have many friends. I barely have time to wipe my ass, much less spend time with friends. You're my very best friend, and now you're leaving, *forever*! What brought about this…this, this, sudden decision?"

"I've already told you. I pretty much didn't have a choice. We're being legislated out of business with all the new endangered species lists, protected species, prohibited species lists. The world is changing. Things just aren't like they used to be. It was and is inevitable. It's not a matter of whether I want it or not, the elephant is in the room, Doc. We can't ignore it anymore."

Lunch arrived. Doc cut a piece of his chuleta and began to chew furiously.

Then suddenly, he asked, "What about snakes? Are they on one of those pinche' lists?"

Andrea's eyes quickly narrowed as she watched Doc.

Brandon said, "What do you mean?"

Doc chewed and talked. "I just know that you brought back a shit load of yellow beards from the Mosquitia."

"Well, we've already shipped those. Besides, we may have lost our prime snake customer."

Doc looked like somebody had tasered him. "What do you mean? What happened?"

"Quintanilla. He's just suddenly dropped off the map. Nobody seems to know what happened to him. Doug heard that he may have gotten cross-ways with the feds for some reason. Probably taxes. I get the impression he didn't keep very good books."

Doc pushed his chair back from the table and tossed his napkin on the plate. As he rose, he said, "I've gotta go. I'm not feeling good."

As Doc turned to walk away, Brandon said, "Wait, we'll take you back."

Doc kept walking and raised his hand in a wave. "No, that's alright. I'll grab a taxi. You two enjoy your lunch." Then he was gone out the door. The waiter approached and asked, "Is he coming back?"

"I don't think so," Brandon answered, a little bewildered.

Andrea quipped, "That went well!"

Brandon looked at her as if she might have some insight as to what had just happened. She didn't. But she felt like she had experienced an awakening. Doc's reaction wasn't just confusing, it was bizarre.

CHAPTER THIRTEEN

New Meaning for 'In Hot Water'

THE DRIVE BACK TO JUNGLE CARGO FOLLOWING LUNCH WAS mostly quiet. Brandon and Andrea were both thinking about Doc's strong reaction to the news, but they were thinking about it from different perspectives.

Brandon was just befuddled and wondering what the hell was going through Doc's alcohol fuzzy brain, a little shocked at the good doctor's response. Andrea, on the other hand was wondering about his intense interest in the snakes. It was so out of character for Doc that she became suspicious there might be more than one layer to Dr. Humberto Dominguez. She decided to have David run a background check on him.

"Nobody seems to want us to leave," Brandon suddenly said as the Jeep made its way down the road.

"Nobody wants _you_ to leave," Andrea replied. "They don't care whether I come or go. They don't know me well enough."

"That was some kind of volcano with Doc. What do you think was going on with him?"

Andrea watched the road ahead. "I honestly don't know, Brandon. Maybe he just sees his partying buddy disappearing. The man does like to carry on a bit."

Brandon laughed. "A bit? The man likes to carry on *a lot*!" he countered.

Brandon's tone changed slightly. "I need to say something…I feel like you're saving my life, Andrea. I couldn't see a way out of here. Secretly, as you know now, I've wanted out of here for a long-long time. But I felt trapped because I didn't know how the hell I was going to make a living. If this thing you're talking about pans out, I could not only make a living, but do something productive with my life, something that's been on my mind since…I don't know how long, but I simply had no idea where to start. So, thank you." He looked over at her and took her hand.

Andrea smiled and placed her free hand on his shoulder. "My pleasure. Which reminds me, I need to nail down a domain name, which isn't going to be cheap, then start building that website, or at least the framework for it. We need lots of material to make it look good; lots of pictures. I'm going to have a camera in your face a lot over the next several days. I hope you don't mind."

"No, it's alright," Brandon said, rubbing the left side of his jaw.

"What's the matter with your face?" Andrea asked, watching him.

"Tooth," Brandon said. "Bit down on a piece of bone at that restaurant a while ago, while I was watching Doc have his tizzy. I think I knocked a filling loose, or something."

"Oh no!" Andrea said.

"It'll probably be alright," Brandon said, tossing it off, and drove on toward the compound.

But it wasn't alright. The pain intensified as the day aged and by bedtime Brandon was placing an aspirin directly against the tooth to quell the throbbing. After tossing and turning until dawn, he gave up trying to rest and got up to make coffee. But that was an exercise in futility. There was no way he could stand the heat of coffee inside his mouth. That was it. He was going to have to go to the dentist post haste.

He got dressed and told Andrea he would be back. She offered to go with him, but he refused, saying it was far more important for her to get on the computer and start doing her thing to create a website. She said okay, so as the sun barely broke into the clear Honduran sky, Brandon Shaw sped away from the compound in a cloud of dust, holding the left side of his face.

An hour later, Andrea was at the computer working diligently to nail down a domain name and start a web page when she heard a car pull up. She rose from the desk, went to the landing and looked down to see who had arrived.

She was surprised to see it was Doc. "Where's the big bwana?" Doc yelled up to her from beside his car.

"Had to go to the dentist," Andrea answered. "He bit down on a bone or something yesterday. He was in misery all night."

"Oh. Sorry to hear that," Doc said as he climbed the stairs. "Why didn't you go with him?"

"Too much to do here," she said. Then she told Doc about building a website and needing a gallery of photos to use on it.

"Wow!" Doc said. "You know, if you want some really beautiful pictures of the forest, has Brandon ever taken you up toward the hot springs?"

"No," she admitted. "He's mentioned it, but so far we haven't found the time to go up there."

Doc was sitting, very relaxed, in a chair next to the desk with his legs crossed. He was acting like nothing had happened to upset him the previous day, and this made Andrea highly suspicious to say the least.

"You know," he said, as if the idea had just popped into his head, "it's a beautiful day…slightly boring, but beautiful. Why don't I borrow a couple of horses from Don Julio next door and let's ride up there? Take your camera. I guarantee, you'll get some photos that are perfect for what you're trying to do."

Andrea was sure Doc was up to something. But what? And more curiously, why? She felt danger very near, tugging at her elbow. But she said, "Sure. Sounds like a great idea. Let me get my camera case and change shoes while you go fetch the horses."

"Ahorale!" Doc said and bounded down the steps to go next door. Don Julio lived nearly a quarter of a mile away, but it was through the coconut forest. There was no way to drive there from here. And that was good, because it gave Andrea a chance to talk to David and see what he had found out about Doc.

When she hung up the phone from that call, she checked to make sure her gun was loaded, then strapped it on in a hidden holster. What she found out was like sticking her finger in a light socket.

When Andrea saw Doc riding up the trail on a horse, leading another saddled horse, she decided to play him for a reaction. "We should wait for Brandon to join us. He ought to be back in a minute."

"Not if he went to see Dr. Jiménez," Doc said casually. In fact, too casually. "That guy is one of only two dentists in town that's worth their spit. And his office always looks like a bus station. If Brandon went in there without an appointment and has to be worked in…shit! You might not see him before nightfall."

"Oh my!" Andrea said, playing along. She climbed aboard the horse that Doc had brought, and they were on their way.

They plodded their way up the path to the main road, then turned left toward Jutiapa, Trujillo and the Mosquitia. Not that they were going that far. They went less than a kilometer before they turned right on a narrow path that led up the side of the mountain. The usually talkative Doc was pretty quiet, only making a comment now and then, mostly about the wildlife including a run-on dialogue about the unusual habits of the Ora Pendula bird, a type of magpie with unusual, comical habits.

After about a half hour of slow plodding, Andrea looked to her left and saw a stream flowing down from the mountainside, making periodic small pools. Those pools were apparently warm because there was vapor slowly rising from them.

Doc commented, "It's almost like an adjustable sauna. The hotter you want your bath to be, the higher up the side of the mountain you go. At this level, the water is a nice, comfortable ninety degrees or so. Would you care to take the waters?"

"No thanks," Andrea said. "Maybe on the return trip." At this point, she stopped her horse, pretending she was looking at something and taking a photograph. The truth was, she didn't want Doc behind her. She maneuvered her horse so that Doc would take the lead.

"About another fifteen minutes," Doc said, "And we'll be at the headwaters. It looks like a caldron from hell!"

"I can't wait!" Andrea said.

Sure enough, another fifteen minutes up the trail and Andrea saw steam rising through the trees and underbrush. She could only imagine what Doc had planned for her, but it was her guess that if he had his way, she would not be going back down the mountainside with him.

Doc's description of the hot spring headwater was very accurate. It was a bubbling, boiling caldron that smelled of sulphur. All of the plants surrounding the roiling hole were dead or wilted for a space of at least ten feet back from the hole.

And, it was dangerous. The hole was not in a flat area, but on a slope. Steam had settled on the ground as moisture condensed in a non-stop, relentless hot bath, so the ground surrounding the headwater was muddy and slick. And this is where Doc chose to find a place and sit, then invited Andrea to join him.

"This is what we came here for?" she said, watching him closely.

"This is it. Well, actually, I wanted you to see the forest on the way up here. It's some of the prettiest and most diverse in the world. Did you know that botanists have come here and said there was no need to go to the Amazon, that we have the same flora right here in Honduras?"

"Is that a fact? And that's what you wanted me to see?"

"Well yes. You said you needed pictures for a new website."

"That's true."

"That website, it was your idea?"

"Yes, it was."

"A lot has changed since you showed up here."

"Is that a bad thing?"

Then Doc's demeanor changed suddenly and radically. He spoke in the same voice, but now the topic began to reveal his plan.

"Yes, it is. Your presence here is causing problems."

"I don't know what you're talking about," Andrea said, now moving away from Doc and preparing herself for trouble.

"I'm talking about an operation that has been running like a well-oiled machine for a very long time, a very profitable operation. Now, all of a sudden, you've got Brandon wanting to bail out, abandon ship, and there's no one else anywhere that can do what he does."

"I see. You mean things like stuff smack down the throats of poisonous snakes?"

"So, you know! Then it's true. You're some kind of a fed, aren't you?"

"What makes you say that?"

"Somebody saw you talking to a gringo in town a couple of weeks ago. A friend had seen him before and knows he's a fed.

There could only be one reason for you to be talking to a fed. You're a fed too, aren't you?"

"Special agent, DEA."

"Goddamn sonofabitch! I knew it. I knew you were trouble the first time I ever laid eyes on you. You're going to arrest everybody in sight, aren't you? Isn't that why you are here?"

"I don't see how that's important right now. The question is, what's on your mind? What are you about to do? What's the *real* reason you brought me here, Doc? It obviously isn't so I can take pictures of posies. You going to kill me?"

"Well, I can't let you fuck up a very profitable operation more than you already have now, can I? I don't have a choice. I've got to make you disappear, then do damage control. You know, it's too bad. Despite it all, I like you. That doesn't make this any easier."

"Doesn't make what any easier, you two faced bastard?"

"Making you disappear."

"And what do you have in mind to make me 'disappear,' Doc?"

"What do you think?"

"You brought me up here to shove me in that hot spring, and then make it seem like it was an accident. Andrea slips and falls into the boiling headwater. Certainly, no evidence to prove otherwise."

"I'm sorry, my dear. It just has to be. Tell me, what happened to Felipe Quintanilla?"

"He's in a federal lockup under tight security. Your drug shipment has been seized. You don't know it, but you assholes are already out of business. And you're next for a trip with handcuffs."

"What the hell are you talking about? I'm a respectable doctor."

"Bullshit. You're the worst kind of evil snot there is, pretending to be one thing, while peddling your poison for profit at the expense of innocent kids dying before they've even had a chance to live their life."

"Who are you to judge me?"

"Society judged you long ago. That's why we have laws."

"You bitch!" Doc snarled and started moving toward Andrea. Andrea backed away. "That was a lot of money," Doc said.

"Too bad. Chalk it up to the cost of doing criminal business. Better keep back, Doc. This may not end well for you."

Andrea crouched down into a defensive stance, and raised her hands in front of her, now ready.

Doc laughed. "Bullshit! How are you gonna stop me?" Doc lunged for Andrea. Andrea sidestepped and pushed Doc away. He fell into a pile of brown leaves but regained his footing quickly and turned to face her again.

Now she was between Doc and the headwater. He smiled an evil smile, as if he had her exactly where he wanted her at last. Suddenly, he charged forward with the intent of striking Andrea and pushing her backward, into the hellish water.

Andrea quickly dropped to the ground like a log. Doc tripped over her body. His momentum propelled him forward and he went headlong into the boiling headwater with a long, agonizing scream. It was over in an instant.

Andrea got to her feet and looked at the boiling caldron. Doc was already dead and blanched a sickening chalk white. He bobbed up and down in the water, being cooked like a lobster.

She couldn't take her eyes off the horrifying scene before her.

Within a few minutes, the flesh began to fall off of Doc's bones, rendering him into a skeleton.

Andrea felt as if she was going to lose her breakfast. She turned away and ran as fast as she could the fifty yards or so back to where the horses were tied. She untied them, mounted one and led the other one by the reins back down the mountain. Her return trip was not as casual as coming up the mountain. She was fleeing. She needed to be consoled by Brandon. But even as she rushed toward him, she wondered if he was aware of Doc's involvement in the drug cartel.

As she rapidly, but carefully negotiated her way down the trail, the vision of the horror she had just seen played over and over in her mind. She had to call on everything she had to suppress losing it and flying into a screaming fit.

When at last, the house was in sight, she saw Brandon on the front deck looking for her. When he saw her, he came bounding down the stairs. She nudged her horse forward a little faster. She needed to feel Brandon's arms around her, holding her, keeping her safe.

At last, she was there. She slid off her horse and grabbed Brandon around the waist.

"I was near frantic," he said. "Where were you and Doc? And where's Doc? I ran into him as I was going into the dentist's office, but he didn't say anything about coming here."

"There's been a terrible accident," Andrea said as she squeezed Brandon with all her mite.

"What kind of accident? Where's Doc?"

She pulled back, so she could look at him. "Brandon, Doc is dead."

Brandon looked like someone had just dropped a bowling ball on his foot. "What?"

"He fell into the hot spring. It killed him instantly."

"Oh, Jesus!" Brandon said, thinking about the fate of Doc. He helped Andrea up the stairs and into the house where she sat on the sofa and told him her story.

"He came here and asked if I wanted to go riding. He said the trail to the hot spring was very beautiful and I could get some good pictures for the website. But when we got to the hot spring, he started talking weird and flipping out. The next thing I knew, he was trying to push me in the water. I dropped to the ground, he tripped over me and went right into the hot water. It was horrible!"

"It's a miracle you're alive," Brandon croaked, taking Andrea into his arms, holding her. "I've always known Doc was weird," Brandon said, "But I didn't think he was a full-blown space case."

"I think he had been drinking," Andrea added.

"So, what's new?" Brandon said. "He was always smashed to some degree. I don't know how he managed to perform in the operating room."

Brandon rose and went to get Andrea a wet warm cloth for her face. Seeing the cloth was like giving her permission. She began to sob.

Brandon started putting things together. "We've got to get rid of Doc's car."

"What?"

"This is Honduras. Accidents are viewed differently down here. They like to blame somebody, no matter what. And I'm not about to let you take a hickey for that idiot's hot bath."

"What do you want to do?"

"We'll wait until a couple of hours after dark, then you follow me in the Jeep. I'll drive Doc's car and we'll park it somewhere near town. There's an old cantina at the edge of town called the Gato Azul. We'll leave it there."

"What are we going to tell the girls? And Lorenzo, Pablo? They all saw Doc and I leave together on those horses."

"I don't know. We'll worry about them later. Right now, we need to worry about what to do with Doc's body."

"Body? There is no body. I watched Doc's flesh fall off his bones in a matter of minutes in that hot sulphur water."

Brandon stared at Andrea, envisioning her words. He grimaced. "Good grief!"

"It was the most horrible thing I've ever seen...or imagined."

"I'm so sorry you had to experience that," Brandon said. She could hear the empathy in his voice. "That must have been a scene straight out of hell."

"That's a pretty accurate description," she admitted.

Two hours after dark, the little two car convoy left Jungle Cargo, headed for town. Forty-five minutes later, they crossed the one lane bridge separating LaCeiba from the jungle road and bounced onto black-top. There was the Gato Azul, on the left. Brandon, driving Doc's car, veered off the road and parked in front of the cinder block building on the far-right corner of the building. Andrea pulled up behind him.

Brandon left the keys in the ignition, the windows down, then, as he got out, he pulled the hunting knife from the scabbard on his belt and punctured Doc's front tire on the driver's side.

As he got into the Jeep, Andrea said, "What did you do that for?"

"To add to the mystery," Brandon said. "The cops will eventually get around to investigating why the car is there. They'll see the flat tire and say, 'well, he abandoned the car because it had a flat'. That fixes his position at the Gato Azul.

"They'll figure he took off on foot to find help and got in trouble somewhere close to here. The Central American mind is very linear."

Andrea pulled out, onto the road, turned right across the bridge and they were on their way back home.

At home, they planned what they would tell the crew, but it didn't appear to be a problem. Everyone took for granted that Doc came and went at odd times, in odd ways. They had all gone home for the night by the time Brandon and Andrea made their nocturnal safari to town. No questions were asked, no inquisitive looks, nothing.

There was a visible sigh of relief. Andrea got around to asking about Brandon's tooth. "I've got to go back today," he said. "The dentist ground the tooth down, he's going to put a crown on it. I've got a temporary thing on there right now."

"Do you need me to go with you?"

"No," he said. "What I need for you to do is stay here and get to work on that website. Are you okay to do that?"

"Yeah, I think so. I'm still a little rattled from yesterday, but I need to get over it and move on. Working on the website might actually help me."

Brandon agreed and left to go to town. Andrea made sure the girls were busy, then made a phone call to fill David in on the happenings of the day before. After that, she got to work on the computer.

Approaching town, Brandon looked and saw Doc's car, still parked in front of the Gato Azul. So far, it hadn't attracted any attention. That was good, Brandon thought. The longer it sat there undisturbed, the better. Then he dismissed it and drove on to the dentist.

He ran into Marta Saldana as he was about to enter the dentist's office. He said a courteous hello, but then tried to avoid the woman and go on his way. But Marta had other ideas.

"Hello, mi Corazon!" Marta said in a come-hither kind of way.

"Hi there, Marta. Good seeing you. Gotta go."

"If you leave too fast, you won't get to hear what I have to tell you about the blonde chinga that you're so in love with."

"No, I won't. Goodbye!" Brandon already had the door open to the dentist's office.

"Okay. Maybe you don't care that I saw her with another man," Marta said, menacingly.

Brandon stopped in his tracks. "What?"

"Oh, *now* I have your attention, huh? Corazon."

"I'm not your Corazon, Marta. Now what are you talking about? Tell you what, never mind. You would try anything, say anything, tell any lie for revenge against a woman you know nothing about."

Marta shook her head. "If you don't want to treat me any nicer than that, maybe I shouldn't tell you anything, or give you what I've been saving for you."

Brandon stopped at the door to listen to what the woman had to say, but he couldn't make himself look at her. "Look, either tell me or don't tell me, but don't try to play your games with me."

"Okay," she said, and turned to walk away. Brandon went on in to the dentist's office and pretty much blew off Marta's performance. Therefore, he was rather surprised when he exited the dentist's office two hours later to find Marta sitting in her car by the curb, waiting for him. He walked over and placed his hands on the edge of the open driver's side window. Marta stared straight ahead.

"What?" he demanded.

"You want my news? Meet me at my house. You want the flims, meet me at my house."

"What fucking 'flims' are you talking about?"

"At the Las Palmas, where she was sitting with the man, she dropped little cans of the flims."

"Flims? What the hell are you talking about, 'flims'?"

"You know. That you put in a camera to take pictures."

"You mean film?"

"Si, whatever you call it. Pelicula. She dropped some cans and I picked them up after she left."

Brandon felt his gut tighten and didn't know why. "Okay," he said. "I'll meet you at your house."

Marta started her car and sped away. Brandon hurried to his Jeep and headed to the last place in the world that he wanted to go.

A few minutes later, he pulled up in front of Marta's small house on a back residential street of LaCeiba. It was painted pink with lots of tropical plants festooning the front yard. He strode to the front door. There was no need to knock. Marta had the front door open. There was a screen door that made it hard to see inside.

"Come in, mi corazon," Marta said with that same syrupy voice.

When Brandon opened the screen door, he saw Marta sitting on her sofa, nude from the waist up, her large, heavy breasts with saucer sized aureoles had no attraction for him now.

"Oh no," he said. "Marta, we're not doing this."

Marta got up from the sofa and clenched her fists.

"You were mine for years before that gringa whore came down here. Now, all of a sudden, you're too good for me? You wants those flims or not?"

"You know what? I don't care. Not that much. Have a nice day, Marta! See you around…or not."

Brandon turned and walked out the screen door, toward the Jeep. From inside the house, he heard a furious scream, then heard the door open and suddenly felt something hit him in the back. It was the rolls of film. He stooped to pick them up and got in his Jeep.

A naked to the waist Marta stood in her doorway and screamed, "My friend told me that man she was with is a federale. Maybe they going to put your ass in jail!"

Then she slammed the door. Brandon went cold all over.

A few minutes later, he was at the same little shop where he and Andrea had purchased the digital camera, talking to the clerk. The clerk was holding the rolls of film. "I can't process them here. Since digital cameras came into use, nobody uses film anymore. We used to keep the chemicals, but they would just get old and spoil. I'll have to send this to the lab."

"Where?" Brandon asked.

"Tegusigalpa, probably. I can have them back here in about a week."

"Damn! There's no place closer that can get it done quicker?"

"I'll make some phone calls, but I'm pretty sure."

"Okay, do what you have to do. But listen, keep this strictly between you and me. Don't call the house when the pictures come back. Don't send me any kind of message. This is strictly hush hush."

"Okay," the clerk said. "Our secret. No problem." Brandon thanked him, shook hands and departed the camera shop.

The drive back to Jungle Cargo was slower than usual. Brandon needed time to think. Marta's revelation had been an exploding bomb in his face, but he also didn't want to overreact.

He knew Andrea was taking pictures of everything in sight, including her photo safari to Sambala. She hadn't tried to keep that a secret from him. Maybe she just ran into a friend, or somebody that was headed to Florida and asked them to deliver the film to a lab up there since, as he discovered, getting the film processed here in Honduras was a problem.

As far as the part about the guy being a federale... hell hath no fury like a woman scorned. Marta Saldana would say or do anything to cast aspersions on the person who she viewed as her enemy. The truth was Brandon had been using Marta almost like a blow-up doll. He had just needed some warm object to occasionally haul his ashes, and Marta was pretty good in the sack, at least better than self-abuse.

So, the likelihood of Andrea meeting with a federale had the extremely strong smell of bullshit. She loved him. He could feel it and see it in everything she did, even to the point of showing him a way out of this frigging rat trap. And what was more, he loved her. For the first time in his life, he had found a woman he thought he could find happiness with for the rest of his days. If there was any chance that what he felt was real, he didn't want to fuck it up by doing what he had repeatedly done in the past and over-react to some cockamamy, harmless situation. It was decided. He sped the Jeep up a little to get home to his woman.

CHAPTER FOURTEEN

A New Problem

BRANDON PULLED UP IN FRONT OF THE HOUSE, BAILED OUT OF the jeep and bounded up the steps two at a time. When he entered the house, he called out to the girls, "Take the rest of the day off. Go home and tell Lorenzo and Pablo to do the same on your way out."

"You mean now?" Suyapa asked

"Yes, I mean now," Brandon answered

"Si, Don Brandon!" the girls answered, threw their aprons on the kitchen counter and went down the front stairs, giggling and chattering.

Naja was lying on the floor beside the desk where Andrea was working on the computer. Both she and Andrea looked at Brandon a little confused.

"How's the tooth?" Andrea asked.

"Never mind that now," Brandon said, reaching out to take Andrea's hand. "Come with me, young lady."

Andrea rose from her chair, following Brandon into the bedroom. "Uh oh!" she said, "This is not going to be 'G' rated, is it?"

"No Mamm, it is not," Brandon said with a small laugh. In

the bedroom, Brandon turned and slipped his arms around Andrea and pulled her to him hard. Then he kissed her, deeply, passionately, and when that came to an end, he kissed her again, like a man drinking from the fountain of love who was dying of thirst.

Somehow in the next few minutes, clothes fell from their bodies like leaves from an autumn tree, leaving them nude against each other, free to feel and react to those electric feelings. Andrea's heat reached a new peak for this jungle man and she gave herself to him inexorably, body soul and spirit. She was his and he could take anything, everything he desired.

And he did desire. He couldn't get enough of this unbelievable woman. In a moment that lasted no longer than the blink of an eye, he thought of what Marta Saldana had said and knew that she was full of shit.

Here was truth, Andrea's perfect body, conformed tight against him with complete love. He could feel it. He bathed his soul in it, let it wash over him and made him feel like at last, he had found a reason for living. He had never experienced that emotion before. Now, he knew the reason he had been brought into this world.

In this magic moment that Brandon and Andrea were joined as one, both tried to push hard enough that their bodies would meld and become a single being. Never had he known anything to compare with this. When their moment arrived, both of them made sounds that were primal, like the first sound that man ever uttered on this earth. Then they collapsed into each other's arms and snuggled as they dozed off into a lover's nap.

Beneath the house, in the carport, Antonio, who had just arrived from the Mosquitia, heard the primeval sounds and knew their meaning. He thought better of disturbing the loving couple and vied for returning later.

The next morning, it was business as usual on the front

deck of the house at Jungle Cargo. All hands were present for the morning repast and get together. The round of questions was slightly different than usual, because the circumstances were slightly different than usual.

Lorenzo asked, "What is going to happen to this house when you go to the United States?"

Brandon sipped his coffee, sat it down on the small table next to his chair and said, "I knew that question was coming sooner or later. As you know, the house is paid for. Hell, you helped me build it. All of you had a hand in it.

"There is not a person here who didn't do something to help build this place, from cutting wood to nailing boards, digging the water well…. Therefore, all of you will become partners in it. I am signing the deed over to all of you. You can all live here. You can decide to sell it and split the money, whatever you want to do."

Lorenzo came to his feet. "Sell the house? Chingow, I would NEVER want to sell the house. Mira! If we sold the house, we would use the money to find some place to live. Why do that if we already have a better house than any land crab around here?" Everybody agreed, verbally and gesturing that Lorenzo was right.

Just then, they all heard a vehicle pulling up in front of the house. Lorenzo went to see who it was and direct them here to the front deck. A few moments later, he returned with Antonio. As Antonio reached the deck, Brandon stood to greet the man.

"Antonio! Welcome. I'm surprised to see you here." Shaking hands.

"I can imagine. How are you, Brandon… Andrea."

"Antonio," Andrea said. "What brings you to Cuyamel?"

"A helicopter, and a rented car!" Antonio joked.

Brandon indicated the table filled with food. "Have you had breakfast?" He asked.

Antonio looked at the bowls of fresh fruit, pan dulce and

other goodies. "No, I haven't. Thank you." So, Antonio picked up a plate and began to select items for his desayuno. Brandon looked at Andrea, then back at Antonio. "We uh, are all a little surprised to see you, amigo. Que paso?"

Although Antonio clearly heard Brandon's question, he remained silent while he made his breakfast choices. Then he moved to a chair at the large, round table, sat and began to squeeze lime juice on his fruit. "We have a situation at the Lost City of The Monkey God. We need your help."

"Me? What on earth for? I'm no archaeologist."

Antonio munched on his fruit for a while, as if he needed time to search for the right words. Naja moved closer to Brandon, as if she sensed something. Her change in mood was not lost on Brandon.

Andrea also moved closer to Brandon. Whatever it was that Antonio was about to say wasn't going to be cause for a celebration. Andrea sensed, as Naja, that Antonio was fixing to drop a bomb.

Antonio sat his fork down on the table, wiped his mouth with a napkin, and looked directly at Brandon. "It is not an archaeologist that we need. It is a translator"

"What?"

"Before I get started, please forgive me, Andrea, but how close are you two?"

"What do you mean by that?" Andrea asked.

"Brandon knows what I'm talking about. How about it, Brandon?"

By now, Andrea had hold of Brandon's arm. "I know what you think you know." Brandon sighed deeply. "Everybody off the deck, go do your work. We need to have a private conversation here."

Andrea said, "Me too?"

"No, not you," Brandon said. "I don't think secrets, any kind of secrets, would be the right thing to do at this stage in our relationship." Andrea thought about Brandon's words and felt guilty about the secret she was keeping.

Meanwhile, everybody scrambled in different directions. The girls went into the house and closed the patio doors. Pablo and Lorenzo went down the stairs, toward the animal compound.

"So, how much does this lady know? Antonio asked.

"Probably almost as much as I do," Brandon answered. "Just what is it that I am supposed to know that she doesn't know?"

"My God!" Antonio said with exasperation. "I didn't know we were going to play this game."

"This is no game," Brandon said, starting to get a little irritated.

"Okay, that unspoken 'thing' you have with animals, to start with." Antonio looked at Andrea. "You ever notice anything a little unusual about how animals react to this jungle man? For instance, let's begin with this, this black jaguar that acts like a goddamned golden retriever when she's around him? Ever been there when someone brought him a sick animal and watched what happens?"

Andrea said nothing, but in truth, she had seen those things.

"What has that got to do with the Lost City of The Monkey God?" Brandon asked.

"That's just the tip of the iceberg, and you know it, Brandon. You yourself have told me stories of how you heard voices of spirits when you were on top of that pyramid in the middle of a rainstorm. Where was it? Guatemala? Tikal? Pyramid of The Giant Jaguar, wasn't it? Inside that temple, trying to get out of the rain."

"That was just one time, and who knows what the hell that really was."

"You know what it was. You KNOW!"

"No," Brandon barked. "I don't. What the fuck was it?"

"That was an ancient Maya spirit trying to reach out to you, to communicate with you."

"What? Come on, Antonio. You've been getting into Didier's jungle juice."

"There are stranger things in heaven and on earth than are dreamt of in our philosophy, Horacio."

There was silence on the deck for at least a full minute. Finally, Brandon asked, "What's all this leading up to?"

"There's some strange things going on at the Lost City of The Monkey God," Antonio said.

"What things?"

"Appearances…. Mayan spirits, apparitions, that kind of thing."

"That's the wildest story I think I have ever heard. But so what? What has it got to do with me?"

"Like it or not, I believe that you are somehow connected to an ancient Mayan legend. 'Legend of the were-jaguar.'"

"That's crazy."

"I've been deciphering some very detailed hieroglyphics that we found on a wall inside of those pyramids. It's even more detailed than the surviving codexes. It details a long story about this man that was either a man/jaguar, or could turn himself into a jaguar. It talks about his giant size. That all fits with the skeleton we found."

By now, Brandon and Andrea were riveted on Antonio's words, but especially Andrea. She was thinking, 'So. That skeleton was not bogus after all.'

"I still don't understand how any of this has to do with me," Brandon said.

"It may not," Antonio admitted. "But then again, it might. It's not like we can do a DNA test to prove it one way or another. But I've known you for years. We're friends, but I've seen some pretty remarkable things when I'm around you. Not just your connection with Naja and being an animal healer, but other stuff."

"What other stuff?"

"You don't remember?"

Brandon was puzzled. "Remember what?"

"You and me were having lunch in Tegus. Remember that place called El Fogon? A drunk got cocky with you, pushed you. The shit hit the fan quicker than the eye can see. You cleared that place in less than a minute."

"How?"

"You roared... Brandon. You roared like a goddamned jaguar. And then you hit the drunk, but it wasn't a hit like a normal hit. It was a... maul. Poor bastard looked like he had a head on collision with a meat grinder."

"I don't remember that," Brandon said.

"Well, just take my word for it. I was there. Scared me so bad I had the shits for a week."

Brandon looked at Andrea. "You sure you want to get involved with me?" Andrea responded by taking Brandon's hand and squeezing it.

Antonio continued. "Brandon, it is my belief, and the belief of some other people who know you, that you might have a chance of reaching across the ... whatever, time/space continuum, spectrum of time, whatever, and somehow communicating, at least to some degree, with these.... these things."

"Whaaat? You must be out of your ever loving, frigging mind. And even if it were true, what the fuck do you expect me to do, ask them if they're having a nice day?"

"I don't think you would have to ask them anything. I think they have something they want to tell us."

"Well, buy 'em a cell phone! This is crazy. Why am I even participating in this conversation? Look, to begin with, if I were to grant this thing any credibility, which I must be out of my mind to even consider, you need somebody that speaks Mayan. That ain't me. And which dialect? Lots of different tribes of Maya, even today. Maybe what you really should be doing is going to the highlands of Guatemala and finding yourself a Quiche' shaman. Didn't the Quiche' write the Popol Vuh?"

"We think they want to communicate with you." Antonio said with resolve.

"Me? You mean me, specifically me? Antonio, I love you, but I think you've lost your mind. This whole idea is unhinged."

"You know that skeleton we showed you?"

"Yeah, the fugaizy? What about it?"

"There's a possibility it was an ancient ancestor of yours."

When he heard that, Brandon rose from his chair and went to the deck railing to look out at the blue water. Over his shoulder, he said, "Antonio, I think you need to go. The bullshit has just gotten a little too deep."

Antonio didn't go. Instead, he joined Brandon at the railing. "I know it all sounds fantastic. It sounds too fantastic to me too. I'm a scientist. We work with evidence. If I find a statue made from stone or clay, that is something we consider evidence. We can analyze it, study it. But there's all sorts of stuff scattered around this site that suggests something beyond the norm was going on there. We've found, for instance, over one hundred stone effigies of what we are calling the 'were-jaguar'. Why? We found the hieroglyphs.

"We found that skeleton that I showed you. We thought it was a glued together fabrication too. But we flew it to Mexico City where some of the world's most highly skilled experts work at the Museum of Anthropology. They've examined the damn thing with x-rays, microscopes, MRI's, chemical testing. You know what they say?"

"What?"

"They say the sonofabitch is real, Brandon. Legit. REAL."

"Well, even if it is, I don't know how you managed to put me into the mix. I'm just a burned-out animal dealer, on his way OUT of the business and on his way OUT of this God forsaken country. You ever hear the term, 'kiss'?"

"What?"

"Yeah, it means, 'keep it simple, stupid'. And that's what I'm gonna do. I'm so close to untangling myself from this misery that I can smell it, and I'm not about to fuck it up in the eleventh hour by getting involved in some crazy, prehistoric lark. Thanks, but no goddamn thanks. It's been good seeing you. Have a nice day! Drive safe on the way back to town."

Antonio dug in his shirt pocket for a small cigar, lit it and took a drag. "Some people who are a lot smarter than me sent me here. People who don't know you personally. That's the reason they sent me. They're willing to pay you a consultant's fee to come to the Lost City of The Monkey God and spend one day. Just one pinche' day."

"To do what? Try to strike up a game of chess with a fucking Maya spirit?"

"They'll pay ten thousand dollars."

Brandon blinked. "Twenty." Brandon sucked his breath in. He couldn't believe he said what he had just said.

Antonio chuckled. "I told them you wouldn't be bought for cheap. Okay, twenty it is."

"I get paid, no matter what. Whether I manage to do any good or not. Whether I manage to strike up a conversation with that 'thing' or not."

"Absolutely," Antonio said.

"And Andrea gets to come along, and Naja. I don't go anywhere without them."

"Of course. Andrea, you are always welcome. Naja too," Antonio confirmed, turning to Andrea, who had also joined them at the railing. "Tell you what, I have some supplies to pick up in town," the archaeologist said. "Also, we need to fill up fuel cans for the chopper. I'll pick you up here, on the beach tomorrow morning, early. There's plenty of room to land out there. We'll fly the three of you into the Mosquitia and fly you back, right here to your front door." Antonio shook hands with Brandon, then Andrea, and was on his way down the steps. A moment later, they heard the rental car start, and he was gone.

"It's a waste of time," Brandon said, looking out at the water as Antonio drove away. "But I'll take their money. We'll need it for the move to the states."

"Are you kidding?" Andrea said enthusiastically. "It won't be a waste of time at all. It will give me the chance to take some absolutely GREAT photos for the web page using the digital camera that we can upload onto the website right away; and the info will go a long way in establishing even more credibility for you. 'Brandon Shaw, renowned traveler and animal expert hired by scientists to consult at Mayan Archaeological site.' That makes for great press, Brandon. Translates to upping your fee for speaking engagements."

"You think so?"

"Of course!"

"I don't know. The word 'expert' has always made me nervous. I was taught that an 'expert' is somebody with a little bit of knowledge, a long way from home!"

Brandon began taking off his clothes and dropping them on the deck until he was naked. "What are you doing?" Andrea asked.

Brandon headed down the steps, barefooted. "Look at that water. I'm going swimming."

"Wait for me!" Andrea yelled and began peeling down to her bra and panties.

CHAPTER FIFTEEN

Return to the Lost City of the Monkey God

ANDREA DID NOT WANT TO MAKE MENTION OF THE FIRST DAY she arrived in Honduras and the scene that played out in The Temple of The Black Jaguar, when she was positive that she had heard not one, but two distinct roars during the brief battle between Brandon and Naja. She did not want to mention it, but it was on her mind.

She packed both of her cameras for the trip, although she wasn't sure why bother with the film camera. She supposed it could serve as a back-up in case the digital camera went on the fritz. Anyway, she didn't have that many rolls of film left, and all that she had exposed, she had given to David, something she almost wished she hadn't done. But never mind! She had managed to pull a rabbit out of the hat and make a deal that indemnified Brandon just as long as she could keep him from doing any more snake stuffing. She was very pleased to discover that he was more than ready to give up that part of his life. It was almost like a miracle.

The bags were packed for an overnight trip, 'just in case,' and Lorenzo had just taken the bags downstairs to the carport when she heard the helicopter approaching. Brandon was giving Lorenzo last minute instructions and providing him with Antonio's satellite cell phone number in case he needed to call. Then, Brandon, Andrea and Naja boarded and were airborne.

As they headed toward their destination in the Mosquitia, Andrea looked down at the winding, dusty pothole filled road below and thought with irony about their previous trip to this jungle.

It had been filled with so many memories, including the death of a young Indian. She could not help but wonder what this trip would bring. And with that thought, came apprehension. It seemed there was always some kind of danger right next to Brandon. Always so close!

As the chopper slowly descended onto its jungle helicopter pad, Andrea, peering out a window was startled to see how many more people were on site since the last time she was here less than two weeks ago. There were people and tents, apparently filled with scientific equipment.

Under her breath, she said, "Oh shit! This is serious!"

When they got off the helicopter, Antonio began introducing them to some of the key scientists and what their fields of expertise were. On the surface, it all appeared very normal, very scientific, but there was an underlying atmosphere of unrest that was thick enough to cut with a knife.

At first, Andrea thought it might be Naja's presence making them nervous. After all, one doesn't normally show up at a party with a black jaguar. But then she started to realize it was something else, something unspoken, but here, and very pervasive.

One other thing that seemed out of place was that Andrea saw no local Indians at work who did the actual manual labor at an archaeological site. Archaeologists say where to dig, and how, but it's always local talent from the available labor pool that does the actual work.

When she asked about this, some man whom she did not

know answered, saying, "They're gone. We just woke up one morning and they had disappeared. Poof! Without a goodbye, kiss my ass, or anything."

"Does anybody know why?" she asked.

"Spooked. We've been seeing some strange things around here. It scared the gee whiz out of the locals."

"What have you been seeing?"

"Not sure. That's the reason some of these ghost hunters are here."

"Ghost hunters?"

"That's what I call them. Their legitimate name is, 'Paranormal Investigators.' More like a bunch of numb nutted freaks, if you ask me. Running around with their little space guns, looking for plasma something-something. It's all highly refined bullshit, if you ask me. People getting paid for nothing."

Andrea smiled at the critic and wondered who he was. But secretly, she kind of shared his sentiments about what she also called, 'ghost hunters'.

The next few hours were rather uneventful. Antonio took Brandon and Andrea into a couple of different tents to show them some of the new discoveries. The various personnel on site all had walkie talkies and would call in from time to time.

"This is Oscar. I just found another one of those werejaguar effigies here in the far south quadrant. Looks like it probably weighs a hundred pounds or more. I'll get pictures."

Andrea turned to Antonio. "How many is that now?"

"Lost count. They're like seashells at the beach. This guy, this…personage, was apparently a ruler, a god, he was king. I don't know what all he was. I don't know if people loved him, if he was benevolent, or if he was a Stalin and they hated him. But I know one thing, he was powerful, and they feared him."

Brandon and Andrea looked at one another.

"I still don't understand what I'm doing here," Brandon said, a little confused.

Antonio stood up from what he was doing, faced Brandon and said, "Right now, you are the single most important person here. By comparison, all these other people are just window dressing."

"Well, I don't know how, and I damn sure don't understand why. What am I supposed to be doing?"

Just then, a frightened sounding call came in over the walkie talkie. "Jade green, jade green. Look for my flare!"

"I think you're about to find out," Antonio said. "Please come with me."

When they stepped outside the tent they had been in, Antonio looked around for a minute and then pointed at a plume of smoke about a quarter of a mile away, caused by a flare gun.

"There!" he said and started walking at a fast pace with Brandon and Andrea close in tow.

Several minutes later, they approached a building that was still in pretty good repair. It displayed all the typical Mayan construction techniques including, as they discovered when they entered, corbelled vaulted ceilings. Doorways had square tops, that were supported by ornately carved sapodilla wood lintels.

There was an archaeologist sitting on the ground just outside the entrance of this building, leaning back against the stone wall. He was breathing heavily and appeared a shade or two lighter than normal.

He looked up at the trio and said, "I'm sorry, but I'm just afraid of that damned thing, whatever it is, and I'll tell you, I advise extreme caution."

Antonio said nothing but ducked inside the entrance which was only about five feet high. Inside, it was dark and gloomy although the archaeologist had set up several portable work lights. The interior was broken into three chambers. They saw nothing in the first one, which was probably an ante-chamber, so they went deeper, into the second chamber, which was about fifteen feet across, from the front wall to the back. Nothing. Just rubble of the ages. Then they made their way forward, into the third and last chamber.

And there it was! A lime green apparition, floating a few inches above the ground. The apparition was a Mayan ruler, attired completely in royal raiment, a jaguar skin cape and loin cloth, a royal bonnet made of quetzal feathers, seashell necklaces around his neck and ankles, his teeth were filed and inlaid with jade, his forehead flattened. In his right hand he held a royal scepter which identified him as a royal personage of high rank. They had the apparition's attention. He could obviously see them. Somehow, he was crossing over the chasm in time from well over a thousand years ago.

"Good God almighty!" Brandon said. Apparently, the apparition could hear and see them also. When Brandon spoke, the apparition looked straight at him with fierce, almond shaped eyes. Suddenly, the apparition's expression changed to one of surprise as he peered at Brandon. His demeanor changed entirely, and he fell on his knees, looking down and extended his scepter toward Brandon.

"What the hell is he doing?" Brandon asked.

"Supplicating himself," Antonio answered. "He obviously thinks he recognizes you. But whatever you do, don't reach out and touch that scepter that he's trying to hand you."

"Absolutely, I will not touch it! Why would I want to do that? There's no worry about me 'touching it'!" Brandon said.

Meanwhile, Andrea was doing her best to not panic. She had the digital camera turned on and was shooting pictures as fast as she could press the trigger. The scene before her was surreal. She felt she must be dreaming. "What would happen?" she heard herself ask.

"I haven't got the slightest goddamned idea," Antonio

answered. "But my instinct tells me, it would be something bad."

"Bad?" Andrea managed. "Define bad."

"How bad does bad get? My guess is, Brandon would be pulled across the time/space continuum into that apparition's world." Antonio said.

"Oh! *That* bad!" Andrea commented, still shooting pictures.

Antonio continued staring at the supplicating apparition. "Maybe I'm full of shit. I've never encountered anything like this before. I'm just guessing. Brandon, are you picking up anything that might be something like a communication of some kind?"

"Communication? What are you talking about? The only message I'm 'picking up' is, we should get out of here!"

"My guess is, this character won't try to communicate with words, but he might try getting some thought process across with… for lack of a better expression, ESP."

"*Esp*? Now, you want me to get chummy with this 'thing' using some San Francisco coffee house bullshit '*esp*'? What makes you think I know anything about *esp*? Goddammit, Antonio! I think you've been getting into the rum bottle a little too heavily, man. The only message I'm picking up is, let's get the fuck out of this place while we still have our scalps. I'm leaving!"

At that moment, the apparition rose from its supplicated position and looked directly into Brandon's eyes with a confused expression. Again, he extended his arm and tried to hand Brandon the scepter. This time, Brandon responded by holding up the palms of his hands toward the apparition in a gesture of rejection.

The apparition's eyes grew wide, then he looked furious and opened his mouth to say something, which was silent to the trio. When Brandon didn't respond to that, the apparition opened his mouth wide in what was obviously a scream, of anger? Of frustration? Of unbridled fury? There was no way to know.

"He doesn't seem to understand why you won't accept the scepter," Antonio surmised.

"Fuck him!" Brandon said and grabbed Andrea by the hand. Then, the trio made a hasty retreat from the building. They passed the archaeologist on their way out.

"Well, what did you learn?" the man asked.

"We learned how to piss off an ancient Mayan spirit," Antonio said, with exasperation. "If I were you, I wouldn't hang around here right now." He followed Brandon and Andrea closely as they made their retreat. The nameless archaeologist took Antonio's harried advice and followed the trio quickly away from the structure.

Back at the central area, Brandon turned to Antonio in a high state of anxiety. "That went well!" he said, as he panted slightly from the fast walk. Naja, as usual, stayed glued to Brandon's side. Perhaps it was her presence that had triggered the apparition's actions.

Several men who had been standing around in the general vicinity started to gather around Brandon. Andrea, seeing this, took advantage of the photo op and started taking pictures.

As if cued, Brandon raised his voice to a level where everyone could hear him and began to speak. "We have just encountered what you folks are calling an apparition. If that encounter is what I was brought here for, then you probably aren't going to get your money's worth. I did not, could not communicate with it. I don't know who you people think I am, but it seems to border on comic book stuff.

"I will tell you this much, however; that 'thing' we just ran into is nothing to play around with. Whatever his mission is, he's serious and it is my belief that he is playing for keeps.

What that means is, he will kill you, and he won't hesitate a second to do it.

"I know you're caught between the devil and the deep blue sea here, what with obligations to grant sponsors and so forth. But…better ask yourselves if it's worth your lives, because in my opinion, that's what is at stake.

"Now, since I have nothing else to offer you, I'm leaving and wishing you well in whatever you decide to do."

He then turned to Antonio and said, "I want you to have that helicopter take us out of here, right now. I don't know what the hell I'm doing here, but I sure don't like what's going on. I'm gonna return to Cuyamel and spend the rest of my life trying to forget what we just saw back there. If your sole reason for bringing me here was to communicate with that thing, it was a bad plan. I'm sorry. I can tell you one thing with absolute certainty, that thing is dangerous. More dangerous than I can put into words. Look out."

Antonio knew there was no need for further discussion. He wrote Brandon a check, wished him and Andrea well and watched them as they boarded the chopper and disappeared over the treetops. Antonio's experiment had failed. He felt as if he himself had failed. He had felt so close to some kind of a breakthrough. Exactly what kind of a breakthrough was unclear, but…something.

He had given his entire life to this study, always believing he would manage to answer some of the questions that have persisted about the Maya for centuries. As the sound of the helicopter faded, he felt complete defeat, and was more sad than he could ever remember having been. His had been a search for truth. Now the truth seemed farther away than ever.

On board the chopper, Brandon didn't bother looking out the windows as they flew over the jungle canopy. He just sat there, closed in. Naja nestled close to him and he seemed to take some comfort in gently scratching her head. Andrea watched him closely. She had never seen him this way before, and for once, she felt there was no way to reach him and offer comfort.

When the chopper landed on the beach in front of Jungle Cargo, Brandon threw his overnight bag out the door as far as he could, then climbed out. He thanked the pilot and wished him a safe flight to wherever he was going, then walked toward the house, picking his bag up along the way. Naja, of course, kept pace with her master.

By now it was dark and once upstairs, Brandon stripped and got into the shower. Andrea joined him. She didn't say anything. Right now, was not the time to talk. They both needed time to process, but especially Brandon.

So, she took turns with him, holding the shower massager and spraying him down, focusing on his back. Thirty minutes later, they were out of hot water, but clean, and feeling a little better.

The day had been too stressful to worry about preparing dinner, so a refrigerator raid was in order. They made snacks of various leftovers, then caved in and hit the hay. Almost nothing at all was said the entire evening, and most certainly no reference to the Lost City of The Monkey God.

CHAPTER SIXTEEN

"Un Incidente De La Selva"

THE FOLLOWING MORNING AT JUNGLE CARGO RESEMBLED normalcy. The entire company met on the front deck for breakfast and a brief meeting. Naja remained close to Brandon's side. Almost too close. It was if she sensed something, although the only outward sign was her protectiveness of Brandon.

Or maybe she was just reacting to his mood. He wasn't really connecting with everybody the way he usually did. He seemed a little distant, even as he munched on bites of fresh mango, his favorite.

After the meeting broke up, Andrea approached him but said nothing. He acknowledged her with a look, then stared out at the sea. A moment later, he said, "We need to get out of here for a while."

"And go where?" she asked, "Into town?"

"No, that's the last place I want to go. Put on your hiking gear. We're going rock hopping up the river bottom on the side of the mountain."

Thirty minutes later, Brandon was walking up the trail toward the mountain behind the house with Andrea flanking him on his left and Naja flanking him on his right. Andrea had thrown together a quick picnic lunch which Brandon now toted in a backpack.

Another half hour and the trio were rock hopping along the river bottom of the Cuyamel river, making progress, but also making frequent stops, either to take pictures or investigate a beautiful orchid or bromeliad attached to the side of a fallen tree. The beauty of the river was breathtaking. The river cascaded down the mountainside creating small waterfalls every few hundred yards with pools beneath the waterfalls.

The sound made by the small falls was most relaxing. Andrea could see Brandon beginning to relax, the farther up the mountainside they climbed.

One waterfall was much bigger than the others and was flanked on either side by curtains of green vines. Dozens of swallows went to and from those vines, obviously having nests secreted within them.

They weren't the only birds. Many parrots flew overhead, noisily chattering as they went. And a large black toucan with a huge yellow bill watched their progress from the treetops. Only, the farther they went up the mountain, the bolder the curious toucan became, getting closer and closer until finally he was in a bush so close that Andrea could almost touch him. She laughed her melodic laugh and talked softly to the bird which drew him even closer. Andrea slowly raised her camera, so as not to frighten the bird, and took a close-up photo of it.

The exploration was at a wonderful, relaxed, casual pace. Andrea managed to get many exceptional photographs, including ones of the toucan. Naja played here like a puppy. She found small fish in the waterfall pools and delighted in watching them dart about. Andrea watched the antics of the big cat and smiled. She had to admit, Naja grew on you. And Naja had shown affection for Andrea by lying next to the desk several times when Andrea would be working on the website. It's like Naja was saying, "Okay, you're family now!"

The air was filled with the gentle aroma of orchids and other tropical flowers, all blending together in a hypnotic medley. Andrea couldn't remember having enjoyed anything so much since coming here. Well, anything outdoorsy, anyway!

Lunchtime arrived, and Brandon picked out a very large flat-topped boulder where they could spread the tablecloth which Andrea had packed. Then she withdrew a good bottle of Claret which was still reasonably cool because she had wrapped it in a towel.

Lunch was u-peel-em shrimp, and an avocado which Andrea halved and sprinkled with lime juice. After a romantic toast, they dug in.

"I love this," Andrea quipped. "We need to do this more often."

"From Florida?" Brandon chided. The lovers laughed easily as they ate and sipped the delicious wine.

Small talk was the order of the day. Brandon explained some of the flora and fauna that surrounded them. Andrea was all ears. "Those bees you see over there are easy to victimize. They have no stingers. Problem is, they don't make very much honey. But they still manage to do their job of pollinating. If you ever get tangled up with a hive, just stand still. They'll go away after a minute or so and you can safely walk away. The reason I'm explaining this to you is, so you don't hurt yourself in a panic."

"Okay," Andrea said, but she was only thinking about how good the repast tasted and the look in Brandon's eyes. He seemed genuinely relaxed, happy, something she hadn't seen much of lately. They chatted a while longer, not worrying about a thing in the world, even laughing about a couple of things. The day seemed perfect. This is how it should be between lovers, she thought. Creating simple, pleasant, wonderful memories.

"Golly," Andrea said with a smile as she reached for the buttons on her blouse. "It's kind of warm today. You think it would be all right for me to get out of this hot top and cool off a little?"

Brandon smiled with pleasure. "Yeah, I think that's a wonderful idea!"

Just then, a metal spear from a spear-gun went whizzing by so close that it nicked the sleeve of Brandon's shirt. It clattered hard against the boulders behind them. As they looked to see where it had come from, they spied a very disheveled Smoke Jaguar peering from behind a boulder about a hundred feet away. His long muslin robe was tattered and badly soiled. He hadn't shaved or cared for himself in quite a while. He seemed unsteady, as if he might have been drinking.

"You runed my life, Jaguar man!" he yelled as he tried to fit another metal spear into the spear gun he was carrying. "Now I gonna rune yores!"

Naja, who had been playing beside a waterfall pool about fifty yards away saw and heard the commotion. She did not hesitate for a second. She bounded over the boulders, closing the distance between herself and Smoke Jaguar in a lightning moment, then launched herself through the air and landed squarely against the ruined cultist. Smoke Jaguar screamed, but that's about all he had time to do.

The impact of the three hundred pound cat hitting against Smoke Jaguar with such unbridled force propelled him backward several feet, landing hard among the boulders. Brandon yelled for Naja to stop, but there was no way she would listen now that she had a chance at revenge against this human beast who had abused and tortured her so badly.

She took Smoke Jaguar's entire head in her mouth and bit down hard. A second later, there was a sickening 'pop' sound as his skull cracked from the force and was crushed between her powerful jaws. Then she proceeded to disembowel him and tear him into pieces. Brandon knew better than to get in her way in this terrifying moment. Andrea held onto Brandon's arm and hid her eyes.

In less than two minutes, it was over. Naja's fury abated as quickly as it had risen once her tormentor lay in pieces among the boulders. The water carried his blood downstream. Brandon called Naja to him. She looked up at her master as if seeking approval for saving his life. This was the one time when Brandon slipped and said something to the cat in their secret language while in front of Andrea. He then called her to him and took her into the pool by the nearest waterfall and washed her all over, making sure he removed all the blood from her.

Andrea watched from the boulder where only moments before they had been enjoying togetherness, and the day. She shook uncontrollably from what she had just witnessed.

"Oh, my God, Brandon! What are we going to do?" she implored.

"About what?" he replied. "I'm not planning on doing a damned thing. This comes under the heading of 'Un incidente de la selva.' An incident of the jungle. Whoever that asshole was, he wasn't local. He won't be missed. Hell, the people of Sambala hated him. The bugs and animals will perform clean-up. It never happened."

"What about his spear-gun?"

"Leave it. Some Indian will come along and find it. Maybe be able to put it to good use. You can bet your ass the Indian will never confess where he found it."

"So, that's it?"

"Yeah, 'that's it'. What do you expect me to do, Andrea? Go waltzing into the police station in LaCeiba and say, 'Excuse me, sorry to bother you, but my jaguar just slaughtered a mother fucker on the Cuyamel River. You'll find pieces of him about two thirds of the way up the mountain, maybe, if you hurry.' I don't need that shit storm and neither do you.

"You want to know the truth? He got what he deserved. Any sonofabitch that mistreats animals, much less tortures them, should, ideally have the same thing happen to them. Call it 'just desserts'."

"Death is pretty harsh."

"*Life* is pretty harsh. The jungle is pretty harsh. Besides, the bastard tried to kill me. That's the second time he tried. And this time, if he would have succeeded, he would have had to kill you because you were a witness."

Andrea blinked at that. She hadn't thought of it that way, but Brandon was absolutely right. "Un incidente de la selva," she repeated.

"Now you've got it. Un incidente de la selva," Brandon said, looking at the remains of Reggie, aka Smoke Jaguar. "And that's how we leave it. The idiot should have learned his lesson the first time he made an attempt on my life."

That part was also true, Andrea thought, as she placed all of their picnic things in the backpack, including the mostly empty bottle of wine. She had let that day at the compound slip her mind.

But Reggie had made a previous attempt on Brandon's life. An attempt that also didn't end well for him. Brandon had a point; he should have learned. Now, her main concern was to make sure she didn't leave anything behind in this place which had been so pastoral. She wanted no trace, no evidence that they had been here.

'Un incidente de la selva'. The jungle had claimed the asshole, in part because he had terribly abused a jungle creature. Life is a circle. Karma. That's how she would file this in her mind.

And now, she turned her back on the shredded remains of the voodoo priest forever, as she walked away beside her man.

Brandon placed the backpack straps on his shoulders, and they began the trip back down the mountainside, almost casually, as if nothing had happened. Naja led the way, sniffing out the trail, being very protective of Brandon, and Andrea too. Naja's midnight black fur glistened in the midday sun. When the sun reflected off her black fur at just the right angle, you could see the outlines of her jaguar rosettes. Funny that Andrea could be thinking of such trivia now.

'Un incidente de la selva,' Andrea thought about this new term she had learned which was more of a philosophy. How apropos. And that is how it ended. The birds flitted about, the orchid's persisted in releasing a most delicate fragrance, and the jungle swallowed what was left of Reggie, as if he had never existed.

CHAPTER SEVENTEEN

"Your Time Has Come, Brandon Shaw!"

THE NEXT SEVERAL DAYS WERE SPENT FOCUSED ON BUILDING the web page. Andrea had almost everything she needed, but she consulted with Brandon numerous times, especially regarding content of his presentations once they started to book. It was clear there would be no problem. The man was an encyclopedia of information when it came to two basic subjects, animals, and the jungle.

It wasn't too big a surprise when two LaCeiba police detectives arrived one day with questions about Doc. Andrea and Brandon gave them blank stares. "What are you trying to say has happened?" Brandon innocently asked.

"That's what we're trying to figure out," answered Detective Enrique Mora. "His car has apparently been parked at a bar called The Blue Cat for several days. But no one at the bar remembers seeing him there. One of his tires is slashed. Could be he pulled in there to get help. But it might have been before the bar was open, or after it was closed, and he took off on foot, started walking, looking for help."

"And he's just disappeared?"

"No one has seen him anywhere. We have been told by

several people that the two of you were good friends. We thought he might have tried to contact you."

"Yeah, we are good friends. I've known him for years. But I haven't heard a thing."

"Well, here's my card and phone number. If you hear anything, please give me a call."

"By all means. Now you've got me worried. Thank you."

The two detectives left. Brandon and Andrea looked at one another. Not one word was uttered, and they went back to work. But a minute later, Andrea couldn't resist saying under her breath, "Un incidente de la selva?"

"Of course," Brandon replied. "What else?"

At last, the web page was ready, and it looked spectacular. Andrea had done a magnificent job. It was a carefully staged concert of photos showing Brandon in a kaleidoscope of situations, holding animals, treating animals. There were pictures of him and Naja. Brandon in his natural element, the jungle. There were pictures of him at the Lost City of The Monkey God, speaking to the gathering of scientists next to the helicopter.

Interwoven, was carefully detailed information announcing his United States speaking tour beginning in six months, and those interested should book ASAP. After showing Brandon the final result and 'blowing him away' with her talent, she opened the web page up, purchased advertising on social media and waited for the bookings to begin.

It didn't take long for interested parties to respond. Almost overnight they had close to a hundred inquiries, people ready to make commitments and back those commitments with deposits. Andrea showed Brandon and it was like someone had lifted a mountain off his back. At first, he couldn't take his eyes from the computer screen. Then, he sagged down into the chair next to the desk, incredulous at what Andrea had just shown him. "This is a miracle. And you are the miracle worker," he said, his voice trembling with appreciation. "I was trapped forever in this dead-end toilet. You've created a path out of here. I owe you."

"No. Let's not predicate a relationship on one of us 'owing' the other anything. What I did, I did out of love. But you know what? It's also a worthy project because you, my man, have a lot to offer the world. What you must tell people is going to draw a lot of attention, and possibly from a lot of important people that have the power to do something about the dangers you reveal to them."

"I never imagined myself doing that. I like it. No, I love it!"

"Your time has come, Brandon Shaw," Andrea said with a satisfied smile.

Brandon smiled to himself.

"It will be quite a change to do something to help somebody instead of," He let his voice trail off. He was also rubbing his left jaw again. Andrea noticed.

"Tooth still hurting?

Brandon nodded. "Yeah, I don't think the crown is seated right, or something. I can feel it when I suck air in. There's a sharp pain. Central American dentists ain't the best in the world."

"Better get yourself back to that dentist before it gets worse."

Brandon started getting up from the chair. "You know what, you're right. I'm going right now, this minute, before this thing drives me nuts. I think it's coming loose, even as we speak."

He bent over to kiss her, then headed for the door, still holding his jaw. As he was going down the stairs, Andrea called after him, saying, "Could you do me a small favor while you're in town?"

"Sure. What's that?"

"I'd like to cook some paella for supper, but I need some saffron."

"I'll see if I can find some," Brandon said.

Then he was in the Jeep and on the way out the front gate.

Andrea turned back to the computer. She felt very content with what she had managed to do. But there was still that one thing that was bothering her which she kept trying to push to the back of her mind. It was reaching the point where she was going to have to address it. Brandon needed to know the truth about who she was.

Or did he?

The truth was she was terrified of what his reaction would be when she told him. Did he really have to know? Did he ever have to know? It was something she wrestled with almost constantly, and she was no closer to divining an answer than ever.

The problem was it had been a big part of her past life. It was bound to surface sooner or later. If Brandon found out other than from her telling him, there was no telling what the repercussions would be. To coin Antonio's understatement, it would be 'bad'.

It felt like one of those rainstorms coming down the side of the mountain. She felt it approaching. Oh, what to do?

In town, Brandon found the dentist's office as much a zoo as always. But he told the receptionist it was an emergency, plus he slipped her a twenty Limpira bill when no one was looking and got ushered into the examination room almost immediately.

An hour later, tooth fixed, he left the dentist's office and headed for a grocery store where he hoped to find the saffron that Andrea needed. Saffron was expensive and sometimes rare but used far more in Spanish dishes than other kinds of cuisine. So, the store had some in stock. He called Andrea to let her know he found her spice, and to see if she needed anything else while he was there. She told him a couple of items. He grabbed them and was at the check-out register when he ran into the owner of the camera shop.

"Don Brandon!" the man said. "Como esta?"

Brandon shook hands with the man. "I'm doing great, Victor. How's business?"

"As good as can be expected. Oh! Your film came back from Tegus."

"Oh, Damn! I had almost forgotten about that. Did they manage to get it processed?"

"Oh sure, but it isn't prints, it's color slides. Can't hardly see them without a projector, or viewer."

"Viewer? Don't you sell those things?"

"I used to. But you know what? I think I have one last one left. If I do, I'll make you a deal on it."

"Sounds great," Brandon said. "I'll be there as soon as I finish here."

As he climbed into his Jeep, his phone rang. Answering, he heard the voice of a very upset Antonio on the other end. "Brandon, your instincts were right, and you were right about those goddamn green things being dangerous."

"What are you talking about?" Brandon asked.

"We're shutting down operations in the Lost City of the Monkey God. We've lost two men already. Everybody is abandoning ship."

"Lost? What do you mean, 'lost'?"

"I mean dead, as in something killed them and we can't swear if it was one of the apparitions or not, because nobody actually saw either death happen; but the evidence is pretty clear."

"Where are you now?"

"I'm on the chopper."

"Do you need a place to stay?"

"Oh, no, thank you. I've got a house in Copan. That's

where I'm headed right now. I just wanted to tell you that your instincts were right. Those fuckers are dangerous. Anyway, we're flying west, to LaCeiba to gas up. I'm not too far from your digs now. As a matter of fact. I just…oh, my God!"

"What is it, Antonio?"

"An apparition is on board the helicopter with us. There's no room in here to get away from the damn thing. It's moving toward the pilot. Oh shit! We're going down! We're gonna…" Then the phone went dead.

"Antonio!" Brandon yelled into his phone. "Antonio? Goddammit! Antonio? Oh, for the love of…"

Brandon hung up the phone and tried to coordinate his thoughts. He had to do something, but where to begin? He started the Jeep and sped toward the airport, running red lights and stop signs. A cop on the corner was yelling at him and blowing his whistle as Brandon blew through the intersection at breakneck speed. In record time, he turned onto the divided esplanade that ran to the airport and the helicopter hanger there. He pulled up in front of the helicopter hanger with a screech of his tires, ran inside and asked, "What have you heard?"

The man behind the counter said, "Nothing. How do you know about it?"

"I was talking to Antonio when his phone went dead," Brandon answered, still out of breath.

"Then you know more than we do," the man answered. "One minute the chopper was on radar, moving toward us smoothly. The next minute, it was gone."

"Where?" Brandon demanded. "Where was the chopper when it disappeared from radar?"

"Over the water, almost even with Sambala," the man behind the counter said.

Brandon tried to wrap his head around all that was

happening. He ran his hand through his hair. "This is a fucking nightmare!"

"What's going on?" the man behind the counter asked.

"You wouldn't believe me if I told you," Brandon said.

"So, what are you people going to do? Just sit around here with your finger up your ass, or go looking for them?"

The man behind the counter looked surprised, as if he hadn't thought of that. "Are you a helicopter pilot?" Brandon asked.

The man nodded yes. "Then what are we waiting for? We need to go look, form a search party, something, dammit, man!"

With that, they ran out onto the tarmac and climbed into the first chopper they came to. A minute later, they were airborne. Brandon was cursing under his breath. Why had it taken him to inspire a search? They should already have aircraft in the air, searching. Dammit anyway! Honduras! Everything in the frigging world is 'mañana' in Honduras.

It only took minutes before they spotted Cayucos in the water at a place close to Sambala. There was debris floating on the surface no more than a hundred yards off the beach. Brandon asked the pilot to fly over the site very low. He opened the door and jumped into the water, swimming to one of the Cayucos and boarding.

"Any bodies?" he asked the owner of the cayuco.

"No," came the answer, "but the water isn't very deep here. We should be able to dive down and see."

"I'll go," Brandon said, and quickly removed his shirt and khaki shorts. He dove in and swam down. Sure enough, he could see the helicopter fuselage about thirty or forty feet down. It would be a stretch, but he thought he could go that deep without a tank.

He had to constantly hold his nose and blow in order to equalize the pressure in his ears, but he made it to the remains of the helicopter. He could see two bodies inside. He tore open the door to the passenger area and snapped the seat belt loose, freeing Antonio's body. He pulled it out of the cabin and swam to the surface with it in tow.

By the time he reached the surface, he was gasping heavily for air. Two men in a cayuco grabbed Antonio's body and pulled him into their craft. Brandon clung to the side, trying to get his breath. As soon as he could, he said, "There's another body down there, but I don't think I can make it."

A young lobster fisherman from the village stood up and began putting on his face mask. "I'll go," he said. "I go that deep all the time to get lobsters."

Brandon said, "Be careful. You'll have to open the door, then unbuckle the pilot. To unbuckle, just pull the latch on the seatbelt."

"No aye cuidao!" The young diver said (No worries). Over the side of the cayuco he went. In the clear Caribbean water, he could be seen swimming down to the fallen chopper. Meanwhile, Brandon managed to pull himself into a cayuco with the help of the owner. Then he turned and sat down to wait for the young diver to resurface.

A minute went by, then two. The diver didn't appear. Another minute passed. Men in the boats began to fidget and mumble and show alarm. Another lobster diver went over the side and swam down.

The second diver surfaced a minute later, pulling with him the dead body of the young volunteer. The minute people saw what had happened, they started to wail. Sambala was a small village and every citizen who lived there was like family.

Cold chills went through Brandon when he saw the dead boy's face. His eyes were wide open and looked as if his last vision on earth was horrifying. His face mask was missing. There was a pall that fell over the small group of men in the cayucos. Silently, they were wondering, but fearing, who goes down next? But Brandon solved that problem for them.

"No one else goes in the water," he said. "We'll wait on the Guardia Coastal to get here. Let their divers hook up cables and pull the helicopter out of the water. Viar para la playa!"

Brandon got on his cell phone and called Andrea to fill her in, thanking his lucky stars that he had decided to buy the waterproof model. Minutes later, she and Lorenzo drove up to where Brandon had beached in Sambala. The rescue helicopter was also parked there.

Brandon asked the chopper pilot if Lorenzo could accompany him back to the hangar and retrieve the company Jeep. The pilot gladly agreed. He also asked if the pilot would please transport Antonio's body to the Mazapan Hospital. That would be the starting point. The authorities would insist on an autopsy. Several men helped load Antonio aboard the chopper.

A minute later, they took off.

A few minutes later, a brightly painted helicopter from the Honduran Coast Guard arrived and started hovering over the site. Then, a coast guard patrol boat came skimming across the water toward the site. There was nothing more Brandon could do. A deep weariness set in. All he wanted to do was go home and bathe, then cave into his favorite easy chair with a relaxing drink and mourn the loss of his friend.

Antonio had been a good person, singular of purpose, Brandon thought. He didn't deserve this kind of an end. Then he thought, it is said that tragedy comes in threes. Was this finally the end of it?

Later, as Brandon sat in his easy chair with a strong cocktail in hand, staring blankly at the wall, Andrea pulled a chair next to him. They both listened in silence to the drums coming from Sambala.

The drums could be plainly heard through the open patio

doors. The wind carried the sound all the way down the beach. They weren't just drums, they were talking drums, telling of the death of a young villager.

They listened for another minute or two. Then, after taking a sip of her own drink, Andrea said, "Do you want to tell me what happened today?"

Brandon continued to stare at the wall, unblinking. "Yeah. But I don't know what happened today. My phone rang as I was coming out of the grocery. It was Antonio. He was on the chopper. He said they were shutting down operations at the archaeological site because two people had been killed and they thought those green things had something to do with it. About that time, he sounded terrified and said that one of those green things was on board the chopper and moving toward the pilot. Then the line went dead. I went to the airport, got a chopper pilot off his ass and we flew to where the last radar report was. There were already cayucos at the crash site, in the water. Thank goodness for that because it made the fallen chopper easy to find.

"I pulled Antonio out of the chopper, but I was unable to dive back down to that depth for the pilot. A young diver from the village volunteered, went down after the pilot and died for his efforts."

Andrea tried to formulate the right words, but that was impossible. Instead, she just sat with Brandon. It seemed the best thing she could do.

"He was a good heart," Brandon said after a half hour. "He didn't deserve to die. Makes me wonder just what kind of a tiger we've got by the tail. For the first time in my life, I feel danger very close to me."

"Tell me everything you know," Andrea posed.

"Everything I know about what? Everybody around me seems to think I 'know something', or that I am something mysterious. I'm just me. I'm just me."

"Well," Andrea said, trying to make him feel a little better, "'me' is one of the most fascinating men I have ever met, or hoped to meet."

Brandon managed a meek smile and took Andrea's hand; but he couldn't get his mind off the death of his friend.

CHAPTER EIGHTEEN

The Pictures

A COUPLE OF DAYS LATER, A FRIEND OF BRANDON WHO WORKED as a pathologist at the Mazapan hospital called him with the results of the autopsies performed on Antonio and the pilot.

No autopsy had been allowed by the villagers of Sambala, who had cremated the body of their lost son.

Antonio had died by drowning. He managed to survive the plunge into the sea from the two hundred feet they were flying above the water. The pilot succumbed from a massive heart attack. "He was probably dead before they hit the water," Roberto said. Brandon thanked him, hung up the phone, then turned and repeated the information to Andrea.

"I want to know what the hell is happening," Brandon mused. "Everything was going so well…so smooth. Now we've got people dropping like flies all around us. Why?" Andrea looked at Brandon. She was empathetic, but she had no answers.

"I think it is far more important to stay on target," she said. She walked to the desk and turned the computer toward Brandon. "In the past couple of days, I have booked over fifty appearances for you."

"Fifty?"

"Fifty confirmed *with* deposits. I've opened a bank account for you in Ocala with the help of a banker friend. Brandon, you have a start-up in your account as of this moment of fifty thousand dollars, and it's increasing by the minute."

"Fifty thousand dollars? What the hell are we doing here? We should be in Florida finding a place to live." Brandon could hardly believe it. He took Andrea into his arms and held her tight.

"It's a miracle. *You* are a miracle!" Andrea smiled broadly as she slipped her arms around Brandon and returned his hug.

Despite the goings-on surrounding Jungle Cargo, business was brisk. The locals, finding out that birds had suddenly taken priority, were happy to accommodate. There had been a steady stream of hunters arriving daily with a variety of parrots and macaws and toucans. Pablo, with some coaching from Lorenzo, was handling the transition very smoothly.

The mainstay bird seemed to be the yellow naped amazon parrot, an above average good talker and fine pet which was much in demand around the world, but especially in the United States. Then there was the blue crowned amazon, a very large parrot which didn't talk quite as much, but they were an exceptionally gentle bird and doted on attention. They made excellent pets. There were tovi parakeets for people who liked a smaller bird, and scarlet macaws for people who liked their birds large. Other varieties filled in the gaps.

Within days, the flight cages were filled to the point of burgeoning. Lorenzo and Pablo had hired a carpenter from Sambala to work full time and trained him to build shipping crates.

The girls were having to neglect their other duties in favor of cleaning cages and keeping the birds fed. This meant that supplies were running short and frequent trips to town were needed for supplies and the ingredients they used to make the birds' food mix.

Everybody was in high gear and very happy because of it. They didn't like the fact that Brandon Shaw was leaving, but now at least, they saw a way they could make a living without him.

At the morning 'front deck meeting', Brandon made several important announcements.

"I've never seen so many parrots in my life! You people have done an outstanding job. Doug is on his way down here this morning. Andrea and I are going to meet him at the airport because we must fly to Tegusigalpa to apply for a broader papel cellado, the export permit you need in order to get these birds out of here and into the United States.

"With luck, we should be back tomorrow morning. By then, you need to have all these birds crated up and at the airport, ready to put on the plane. We have got to have an exact count and inventory, meaning how many of which kind. That means you're going to have to segregate different species of birds into different flight cages. It's going to be a huge shipment and every one of you are in for a big bonus."

Everybody cheered.

"Now, beyond that," Brandon continued, "I had a long conversation with Doug last night. The final decision is up to you, of course, but; we are pleasantly shocked by the number of birds being brought into Jungle Cargo. The point is, there are enough that 'if' you decide you want to keep Jungle Cargo alive and operating, Doug is open to that. The company would operate more or less as before, but exclusively with birds. No snakes, no primates, no coati mundis, etc. Puromente pajaros! Do you want to do it?"

The crew, including the new carpenter, all started yelling and cheering in unison, and dancing around on the deck.

Brandon let them cheer for a minute, then calmed them down.

"Okay, okay, calmase! Now, you have to understand that I am still leaving. This wonderful woman who came to us a while back," he indicated Andrea, standing next to him, "has developed a way for me to make a living and perhaps still help Jungle Cargo from a public relations standpoint. Odd as it sounds, I might be able to do more good for you from the United States than if I stay right here."

Brandon spent the next half hour explaining the web page and what it had resulted in, then showing each one of them the page on the computer. They didn't completely understand, but they were trying. Andrea took over and had better luck.

"The point is," Brandon said, "You aren't really losing me. Like Doug, I will be operating out of Gainsville, but I will still be in fairly close touch. Lorenzo, Pablo, Anna Maria, Suyapa, you are all equal partners in the new Jungle Cargo. I have called my lawyer, Vicente, and he is drawing up the legal documents to make you the owners, even as we speak. That means, this house, the Jeep, the blue truck, all the tools and equipment, they are all yours."

"What about Naja?" Lorenzo asked.

"Where I go, Naja goes," Brandon said. "She is not part of the deal."

"Oh, thank goodness!" Lorenzo said, sounding relieved. "I would not want to have to deal with her if you abandoned her." Everybody emphatically shook their heads in agreement.

The meeting broke up, but very up-beat. There was elation and excitement at the announcement that they could keep Jungle Cargo alive and operating. It was like keeping their family together.

Brandon and Andrea packed an overnight bag, bade everyone goodbye and drove to the airport to meet Doug and the plane.

Not that it mattered but traveling to Tegusigalpa shouldn't have been necessary. It was a bureaucratic piece of paperwork that should have been able to be handled over the internet, except for one thing. This was Central America. And in Central America, the thing that moves paper across the top of a desk is the paper that moves underneath the desktop. It's called 'mordida', a polite word for pay off. So, the only reason for going to Tegus was to pay off the minister of natural resources so he would approve the new export permits and then pay off his secretary, so she would type them up once her boss had given her the order.

All of that should take no more than a couple of hours, then they would be on their way back to LaCeiba. By then, Lorenzo and Pablo would be waiting at the airport with the load of parrots, and they could get on with life. The time drew closer for Brandon to break away from Honduras and make his move to Gainsville. The thought of it filled him with exuberance. It's like his life was starting over again…a renewal! He was also secretly a little frightened of entering this new life, but with the map that Andrea had managed to lay out, it was all so logical that real fear had no place.

Everything went like clockwork in Tegusigalpa. They returned from Tegus to find the old blue truck waiting outside the gates. The truck gained entrance, they immediately loaded the parrot crates onto the plane and Doug was ready to go in record time.

Just before Doug climbed aboard to take off, Brandon told him, "The next time you come down here, Andrea and I are going back with you. I have a little more training to do now that we have decided to keep the company operating, but then I'm ready to go. Andrea is already scouting houses in Gainsville via the computer. Modern communications, huh!" They shook hands and Doug was taxiing away before Brandon could get the Jeep started.

This had been a record setting load and there was reason for celebration. Actually, there was more than one good reason to celebrate. Unlike other previous loads of the past few years, this load was completely legal, and that was a damn good feeling!

Brandon gave Lorenzo a list of party things to buy before returning to the compound. It was a list Lorenzo gladly accepted. He and Pablo would make the stop and load up.

There was a celebrative mood at Jungle Cargo that night. Brandon had Lorenzo and Pablo build a bonfire on the beach and a trio of singers were hired to come out from LaCeiba to entertain. Everyone at Jungle Cargo was celebrating as well as Don Julio, the neighbor, and his family. Brandon had also invited the families of Lorenzo and Pablo, as well as his banker to join the festivities.

Music played, the flames leapt high on the beach from the bonfire, and Brandon and Andrea danced barefooted in the sand. The girls giggled and dared to take tiny sips of the Flor De Cana rum. Lorenzo sat on a log talking to the neighbor.

The only person who looked out of place was Pablo Palma. In fact, his mood was downright dour. So much so that everyone avoided him and left him to his own devices, although no one could figure a reason for him to be less happy than the rest of the company at Jungle Cargo.

He sat off to one side and drank Agua ardiente, a local moonshine that tasted more like kerosene than alcohol.

The party started to wind down about one in the morning. The compound was devoid of livestock, so Brandon told everyone to take the day off. That way they would have time to recover from their hangovers. As for himself and Andrea, they took a long shower together, and then enjoyed each other, together.

The next morning Brandon was making busy in the kitchen creating omelets. But this was not all that was on his mind. As he and Andrea sat at the breakfast table, he brought up the subject of their relationship. "You know," he said, "We have never really sat down and confirmed our relationship beyond here. I hate to assume anything."

"Go ahead and assume all you want," Andrea said. "We are a couple. We'll be a couple until you run me off, which I hope will never happen. There. Satisfied?"

Brandon blinked. "Satisfied!"

"End of topic! Let's eat, I'm starved. I think it's all that 'exercise' I'm getting at night!" They smiled at one another, then devoured the omelets.

Later, Brandon walked out on the deck, as was his habit, to gaze out at the sea. It was almost his way of sticking his finger in the air to test the direction and speed of the wind.

He was a little surprised to see Pablo Palma, still on the beach, apparently passed out from drinking too much agua ardiente. Normally, he would have gone down there to check on the man, but considering Pablo's unexplained bad mood, Brandon decided to leave him alone. Andrea appeared at Brandon's side and saw what he was looking at.

"What's he still doing down there?" she asked.

Brandon shrugged. "Good question. Don't know. Who cares?"

They walked away from the deck railing and into the house. Andrea checked the computer, then announced, "We have thirty-two more inquiries about you making a personal appearance. If I collect a thousand-dollar deposit from each of them, you're going to be solidly booked for more than a year."

"Amazing," Brandon said. "Just amazing. Let's just hope I don't disappoint."

"You could never do that," Andrea said with a smile. "What I'm imagining is, people will have a hard time staying in their seats when you start speaking and showing them pictures of the jungle."

'Pictures!' That reminded Brandon that he still hadn't retrieved his pictures from the camera shop in town. Somehow, the importance of them had diminished by now, but he still had to pick them up at some point. Also, his tooth, which was still sore, reminded him that the dentist had written a prescription the other day which, because of everything that happened from the moment he walked out of the dentist's office, he neglected to get filled. The throbbing in his jaw reminded him and made him wish he had the medicine.

"This damn tooth is hurting," he told Andrea. "The dentist gave me a prescription the other day that I really need to get filled. Want to go to town with me?"

"I'd love to," she said, "but I think I need to stay here and respond to these inquiries. We need the nest egg. If they pay the deposit, we'll have over eighty thousand dollars accumulated to begin our new life."

"Sounds like a good reason to stay here," Brandon said with a smile. He kissed her and bounded down the steps. Glancing to his right, he saw that Pablo Palma was gone and assumed he had made his way down the beach to Sambala. Whatever. He couldn't worry about Pablo Palma right now. He jumped in the Jeep, started the motor, steered out the gate. He wanted to get this over with as quickly as possible.

In town, Brandon had to get the dentist to re-write the prescription. The original had gotten wet and munched in the wet bottom of the cayuco that day at sea. From there he went to the pharmacia and got the prescription filled. He was in pain, so he bought a soda pop and downed a pill. Then he jumped in the Jeep and started back to Jungle Cargo. As he drove down the street, he passed the camera shop and remembered the film. He pulled over to the curb and went in the store.

The clerk saw him coming and retrieved the processed film, which was color slides. He also found the final slide viewer he had in the store. "As promised, I made you a deal on the slide viewer," the clerk said with a smile. "Fifty Limps for everything."

"Fair enough," Brandon said, digging the money out of his pocket. "So, how do I work this thing anyway?"

"Very easy," The clerk said. He opened the box, then opened the battery compartment of the slide viewer, inserted some batteries and flipped the viewer over. Then he opened the box of slides, turned them the right direction and put a stack of them in the tray. "Okay, all you do is pull this little slide tray out, then push it back in and it will feed one slide at a time into the viewer. A light automatically turns on inside the viewer when a slide is ready to view." He demonstrated the process, which placed a slide in the viewer and lit up the small screen. He handed the viewer to Brandon.

Peering into the viewer, it took Brandon a moment to focus. When he did, he went pale. Shaking visibly, he changed to another slide. There he was in close-up and living color, maneuvering a sealed bag of smack into a snake's throat. He went to the next slide; more damning evidence against him.

By the time he had looked at all the slides, Brandon Shaw was in shock. He took his viewer and slides and staggered out the door of the camera shop. Climbing into the Jeep seemed a struggle. His legs felt like they were made of lead.

After he was seated in the Jeep, he just sat there for a long while, trying to collect his thoughts. He reached under the seat of the Jeep and pulled out a bottle of Flor De Cana rum, then drank deep from it.

Suddenly, all truth seemed kaleidoscopic. What the hell was the truth? Who was Andrea Granger? He had thought she loved him. Was this whole thing just a set-up to nail him? There was only one person with the answers, and he wanted those answers. He needed those answers. He needed to know if he was a patsy, walking into some perverted kind of elaborate trap. He started the Jeep and headed for Jungle Cargo, drinking the bottle of Flor De Cana as he went.

By the time Brandon pulled into Jungle Cargo, the pill and rum had mixed. Brandon was well under the influence, something Andrea, who was waiting for him on the back veranda, wasn't prepared for. He intentionally left the slides and viewer hidden in the Jeep for the time being.

It was all he could do to ascend the steps. It was all he could do to put one foot in front of the other until he arrived at the landing. When he did, Andrea was there, waiting for him with a kiss. He kissed her, but it was lack-luster, and she immediately sensed it. As he walked on past her, into the house, she was puzzled. "What's the matter?" she asked.

"It's been a rough day," he replied.

"You've been drinking."

"Oh, yeah. Did I not mention that? I've been drinking. Boy have I been drinking!"

"Any special reason why?"

"Seemed like the right thing to do." Brandon stopped by the liquor cabinet, grabbed a bottle of rum and went out of the house through the front patio doors. He said two words to Naja who was spread out on one of the chaise lounges. They were words unlike anything Andrea had ever heard, and whatever they were, Naja sprang to her feet and positioned herself at Brandon's side in a posture that meant she was guarding him. The hair went up on her hackles and she issued a small roar. Then she and Brandon went down the steps to the front yard, walked to the beach, turned left and walked west, out of sight.

Andrea was perplexed. There was clearly a problem, but she was at a loss to know what it was and now was certainly not the time to try and approach Brandon to find out. In fact, now that she had a moment, she sucked in air and felt fear because this was the second time she had seen evidence that Brandon had some 'secret' language he shared with the black jaguar. Whatever it was, it was commanding and Naja understood every word of it.

There was after all, a secret part of Brandon Shaw that lived just below the surface of the one he showed the world, whether he wanted to admit it or not. Suddenly, Andrea was frightened to know who that other Brandon was.

Brandon's unexpected mood had shaken her up. She grabbed a wine glass and went to the refrigerator where she retrieved a bottle of rose' and poured full. Up until the moment Brandon had arrived, it had been an exciting, successful morning. She had received deposits from almost everyone who had made inquiries on the web page. There was now well over eighty thousand dollars in the bank account. Brandon's future was secured. He was booked for well over a year. She was having to send out notices that there would be a waiting list for all other people wanting to hear Brandon Shaw.

But now, she stood at the railing and watched furtively for her man to return from his walk down the beach.

CHAPTER NINETEEN

The Showdown

I T WAS LATE AFTERNOON WHEN B RANDON AND N AJA reappeared on the beach, then turned and walked across the front yard to the front steps. "Let's talk!" he said to Andrea, as he stepped onto the landing of the front deck, rum bottle in hand, now nearly empty. He walked past her into the house.

"Good idea," she said, following him with her eyes. As she followed him into the house, she said, "Would you like some dinner?"

"Dinner?" Brandon said, pausing. "Dinner. Yes, dinner sounds like a good idea. That would explain that gnawing in my stomach. Yes, by all means. In fact, dinner and a show!"

"What?" Andrea asked.

"Oh, nothing. Just a little joke," Brandon answered. "It's an old saying. You know, dinner and a show." Brandon went into the bathroom to wash up, then returned to the living-room and flopped into his favorite chair.

As Andrea prepared dinner, she said, "Great news! I confirmed all those inquiries today, and accepted deposits from them. Brandon, you're booked up for over a year!"

"It sounds too good to be true," Brandon said. "So, tell me, Darling, is it really true?"

"What an odd question," she said, looking at him for some hint of what was on his mind. "Yes, of course it's true. Why do you ask? Well, never mind. I think I understand."

"Do you? Well, that's good. Then maybe you can help me understand."

Andrea didn't respond. She was waiting for the other shoe to drop. But Brandon left it hanging there. He struggled to his feet and walked out to the railing to catch the last rays of sunset. The sky was tuna pink. Far offshore, and slightly to the right, one could see the Cayos Cochinos Island group.

Dinner was disturbingly quiet. Andrea wrote that off to Brandon's state of inebriation. She hoped some food in his stomach might absorb some of the alcohol and help him on the road to recovery. But it was still a mystery as to what had set him off to begin with.

Somehow, the normal sounds of forks and knives against plates seemed loud. It was now dark. The songs of tree frogs filled the night. Andrea loved their symphony and found solace in them. Eventually, Brandon finished eating and said, as he pushed back from the table, "Very good. Thank you, Darling. Well, now I think it's about time for the second half of tonight's entertainment. I'll be right back!"

He managed to get to his feet, still unsteady, and make his way to the back door. She heard him clomping down the stairs as she cleared dinner dishes away and put them in the sink. Brandon reappeared a minute later with a paper sack in his hand. Andrea was becoming more puzzled, but also more apprehensive.

Then, Brandon sprang his surprise. He pulled the slide viewer from the paper sack, then the box of color slides. He looked at Andrea and said with a twisted smile, "Dinner and a show!"

He removed the slides from the box and placed them in the viewer tray, then inserted one of them into the viewer, turning on the viewing light inside the machine. He then handed the viewer to Andrea.

She took the viewer from his hand and peered at the screen. There was a close-up of Brandon stuffing a snake with drugs. There were other slides, but she didn't need to see them. She knew she had been caught.

"Oh, God!" she said over and over. "Oh, my God! You want an explanation?" she said, trying to push her tears back.

"An explanation? Yeah, an explanation would be a good thing," Brandon said. "Do you have an explanation? A truthful one?"

Thus cornered, Andrea proceeded to give Brandon a truthful and detailed, explanation.

"Gainsville is a college town, as you know. The sudden influx of heroin there was causing big problems. Kids were overdosing, dying, a lot of pressure was brought to bear. Important people wanted to know where it was coming from and stop it. So, we were brought in to investigate."

"We? Explain 'we'."

Andrea hesitated for a moment, took a deep breath and finally said, "Brandon, I'm with the DEA, or at least, I was. I was assigned to get a job with Doug because it seemed like Jungle Cargo had something to do with the sudden influx, somehow. We just couldn't figure out how. It became obvious that Doug didn't know anything, so they told me to come here. This, it seemed, was the trouble spot. And…as it turned out, it was. But then, things became very complicated, and I have to take responsibility for that."

"Complicated? Explain, 'complicated." Brandon sat with his fingers interlaced and his legs crossed, watching Andrea's every move.

"I broke a cardinal rule. I fell in love, for the first time in my life. And the person I fell in love with was the person I was investigating." Andrea started to sob, but got hold of herself, wiping away her tears and continuing.

"I had the evidence I needed to arrest you. But instead, I made a deal with my boss to bring down everybody around you and leave you out of it. You are really a small player anyway. You were being used, Brandon. They used you because of your unique talent with animals as a way to get their poison past customs agents. Believe it or not, you were as much a victim as anybody."

"How do you figure that?"

"You were being manipulated. Everybody knew it. And Lord knows who all was in on it. You were surrounded like a wounded bear. That day that Doc showed up here. He took me up on the side of that mountain to kill me."

"What?"

"He's been a part of the cartel the whole time. Well, he *was* a party to it. Reggie is another one that knew. He's the one who took me to the poppy field. You know him as Smoke Jaguar. He told me how he blackmailed you into loaning him Naja."

"His real name was Reggie?" Brandon started to laugh.

"But the real bastard in all this was Felipe Quintanilla. He's in jail, no bond, incommunicado until his trial. The only person he can talk to is his lawyer."

"Well, that's a good place for the asshole," Brandon said. "I never could stand him. Money makes you get in bed with some strange people. The last time he came down here, I told him never again. I was getting out anyway."

Andrea thought back for a moment. So, her 'dream' hadn't been a dream after all. So, if that hadn't been a dream, what about the jaguars in the garden at the Jungle Inn?

She kept going. She had to get this all out now that she started. In a way, she was glad. She had been holding it inside for what seemed like forever.

"Everything was going well. Quintanilla is in the slammer. The poppy field has had herbicide sprayed on it and those clowns that worked in the 'factory' have been arrested. And then, a true miracle happened. I saw a way to free you from the need to ever transport drugs again. And you've already admitted, you were ready to quit. But even before you ever said it, I saw it in your eyes."

"Yeah, I admit it. It was like somebody cut me free of chains."

"Yes, well, that may be a lot closer to the truth than you know. By the way, where did you get this film?"

"You apparently had a meeting with some blond-haired man. You were giving him a bunch of rolls of film and dropped a couple. Your old arch enemy, Marta Saldana was watching you and grabbed the film when you left from wherever you were."

"Hmmm, Marta. She would do anything to cut my throat."

"Understatement."

"I wanted to tell you so badly. I've been trying to figure out how to tell you for weeks. I just didn't have the courage. I really love you, Brandon. I don't want to ever hurt you. As a matter of fact, I've done a lot to keep other people from hurting you. Now, I want to ask you to forgive me. Forgive me for keeping secrets from you."

Brandon stood up from the table and walked to the fridge for something to drink. He didn't say anything for a long time while he processed everything Andrea had just confessed to him. Admittedly, there was a tug of war going on inside him. But for once in his life, logic was winning over from pure, raw emotion, perhaps for the first time in his life; more proof of the influence this amazing woman was having on him.

Finally, he returned to his chair and after taking a long drink of his soda, he said, "I'm not sure there is anything to forgive. You saw a flawed man and instead of sending me to hell, which you clearly had the ability to do, you came to my rescue. You saved my life. And now, you stand there humbly and ask me to forgive you? There's nothing at all to forgive. Just promise me one thing, no more secrets from this point forward."

"Oh, God, yes. I promise," she quickly said. "But tell me, can you promise me the same?"

"What do you mean?" Brandon asked, taking a sip from his soda pop.

"Can you promise me to not keep any secrets from me?"

"About what?"

"About who you are."

Brandon took another deep sip from the soda pop. "I'm not sure I know who the fuck I am anymore."

"Well then, can we work on finding out together?"

"Slowly. Don't push it."

Andrea looked down. "I guess I'll have to settle for that, for now." Then she stood up. "Okay, Brandon. You have my promise. No secrets, no lies. I am yours, completely."

"I'm happy about that, but what's the deal? Are you going to continue working for the DEA?"

"No. Part of my agreement was, in return for them granting my favor, I'm being forced to throw in the towel. I've violated just about every rule and code of conduct in the agency. I've got to take early retirement. I've violated policy, to say nothing of tenet. But you know what? I don't care. It doesn't matter. It looks like I have plenty to do as your agent and partner."

She paused and looked at her man. "Brandon, we can have a good life together, if that's what you want."

"Yeah, I want. I can't think of anything I have ever wanted as much as this."

He paused. Then, "So, you sacrificed an entire career for me?" Brandon said with a half-smile.

"That just goes to show that what I have come to believe is true," Andrea said with a sheepish smile.

"Yeah? And what's that?" Brandon asked.

"That true love is a force strong enough to move any mountain."

"True love," Brandon repeated. "I never thought about it before, but I guess you're right."

The moon was rising, and Brandon casually walked out on the deck to look at it. He was still unsteady from his day of bingeing and thought some fresh air might help.

So, it was that he was completely unprepared for what happened next. The jade green apparition of the Maya chieftain manifested itself to his right. He didn't notice it at first, then, when he did, he said with disgust, "Get the hell out of here! I don't have time for your horse shit!" He then swung at the green thing as if he could hit it or brush it away.

But crossing his hand into the green field is the last thing he should have done. In an instant, the apparition transferred itself inside him, and was seeing through his eyes. Brandon was no longer in control. His body had been taken over by the prehistoric Mayan.

Brandon stood motionless for a moment, then the Mayan turned this human body and walked back into the house. From the kitchen, Andrea saw him coming, but didn't realize what had happened. Instinct told her, whatever it was, it was very bad. She reached for the phone and pressed the 911 button, which alerted David Harkness that a major problem existed.

The possessed Brandon approached Andrea, then spoke to her in an ancient Mayan dialect. After that, he backhanded her, hard, knocking her half unconscious.

Before she could fall to the floor, he reached out and caught her, cradling her in his arms; then, moving like a robot, he walked to the back door and down the steps, toward the animal compound.

Brandon, possessed, walked straight toward the snake pit. Andrea began to regain consciousness and tried to struggle, but it was no use. Brandon, or whoever this was, was far stronger than her.

Moments later, Brandon laid Andrea on the parapet of the snake pit and prepared to push her in. It was at that moment that somebody approached him from behind and hit him hard on the head with the only weapon they could find, a large green coconut. A primitive instrument, perhaps but it was heavy, and effective. It knocked Brandon to his knees.

When he fell forward, he landed hard against Andrea, pushing her over the side of the parapet into the snake pit. He then managed to turn to face his attacker. It was Pablo Palma, who was preparing to hit him again. By now, Brandon's vision was in vignette, but he saw a large jaguar paw come into his field of vision and swipe with lightning speed at Pablo Palma.

There were screams, and blood gushed from Pablo as he grabbed at his face and neck. Then the claw appeared a second time to finish the job. After that, Brandon passed out. All was silent. All was black. All was peaceful.

Sirens could be heard coming up the main road from LaCeiba. Several cars and other service vehicles were all in convoy to Jungle Cargo resulting from Andrea's success at pressing the panic button.

Close to a dozen vehicles skidded to a stop in front of the house with teams of agents disembarking, guns drawn, prepared to face whatever beast awaited them. None did.

It was hard to tell what all had happened in the darkness, but they did find the body of Pablo Palma, ripped to shreds. David searched frantically for Andrea and finally called in a helicopter to provide light. Eventually, he found her. She was sitting on the parapet of the snake pit, looking a little disheveled, but none the worse for wear. David immediately went to her to ask what had happened.

"That's going to be hard to answer," she said. "Let's wait until I get a little more composed, and for the light of day."

And wait for the light of day, they did. David helped Andrea back up the stairs, into the house and kept asking, "Where's Shaw?"

"I'm not sure," Andrea answered honestly.

"I need to know what happened out here," he kept saying. "This place is a mess. We've got a dead body, and I don't mean just dead, but sliced up like bacon. Who's responsible for that?"

"Has to be Naja, the jaguar," Andrea said.

"Fuck me! You mean there's a jaguar running around out there somewhere, and I've got men who might walk up on it?"

"They might," Andrea admitted.

"Shit!" David said, and went to the door to warn everybody to call off any search until daylight. He immediately got on his walkie talkie. "Signal nine, signal nine! Retreat and call off the search until we have full daylight. There might be a —they're gonna love this—a damned jaguar hiding out there someplace."

When dawn finally arrived, David Harkness walked back down into the compound and searched for clues. What he found were tracks, lots of them. Two sets, those of a man and those of a big cat, went toward the beach, then turned right and disappeared into the jungle. It was David's job to follow them and look for his suspects.

He did so for several hundred yards, but then he encountered a terrifying problem. Blocking the trail in front of him was a jaguar. It wasn't Naja. This one had rosettes, but it was huge. It didn't try to charge him, but rather just sat in the middle of the trail and opened its mouth with a thunderous roar, in warning.

David pulled his Glock. He was taking no chances. But then he looked again and realized that jaguar was not alone. There were other jaguars who slowly emerged out of the underbrush, dozens of them. They all took up position in a line, sat and made it clear that no one was going beyond that point.

David got the message quickly. He backed away slowly, muttering under his breath. His hand was shaking so badly that he could barely hold his gun.

"Oh, dear God, get me out of this and I'll go to church every Sunday the rest of my life. I'll give up smoking, cursing."

He held his Glock in front of him in a firing position, but he was painfully aware that he may as well have a BB gun.

There was no way he had as many bullets as there were jaguars, even if he assumed that every shot was a kill shot, which was highly unlikely. If these cats bolted, it was his ass.

He did not stop backing for fifty yards, then he turned and walked ever so briskly back to the house at Jungle Cargo. When he got there, he was babbling and shaking like an out of balance washing machine.

"Thank you, God! You, you, you wouldn't believe what I just saw!" he said to Andrea in a terrified, quavering voice. "There were jaguars, dozens of them, I mean, *dozens* of them, all in a row! I thought I was a goner!"

Had it been another time, another place, Andrea would have doubted David's words as the ranting of a mad man. But she had been here long enough that she knew anything was possible. And she hoped anything was, because right now, her heart was breaking. Had Brandon gone down the beach, escaped, never to return?

She left the safety of the house and walked down to the beach. She saw the tracks that David had followed. She stared in the direction where those tracks went. A deep sadness came over her and tears welled up in her eyes. She stared for several minutes, then started to turn and walk back to the house.

She felt totally lost, defeated, one part of her just wanted to die. She had been so close to making this work. The pain was tearing at her heart.

Then, she changed her mind about going to the house and instead, she retraced David's footsteps, not caring in this moment if the jaguars were still there and if they wanted to kill her. That would be fine with her, because without Brandon, her reason for living had evaporated.

She walked aimlessly for five minutes and finally did encounter the jaguars. But in the inimitable way that animals have, she understood that they would not hurt her. She approached the big one in the middle of the path and gently stroked it on the head. But her tears stopped her. She had lost Brandon to whatever contrivance, and with him, her heart, and her hope for ever being happy. She slowly turned, like some animated doll, to walk back to the house.

Then, in that final moment before returning, she heard a familiar voice. She couldn't understand what that voice was saying because it was speaking in a very secret language. But it was enough to make her freeze in her tracks.

A minute later, Brandon Shaw appeared on the trail, Naja at his side. Both were sauntering at a casual pace, as if it was just another day at the beach! Whatever he was saying to Naja, it sounded a lot like an ass chewing. Then he looked up and saw Andrea. He stopped a moment, smiled and came toward her, walking a little faster than before.

"You're alright?" he said as he approached. "I thought you were injured, or worse."

"Why?"

"The snake pit. I could see things, but I couldn't stop them. I had no control."

"Oh, the snake pit! Well, you told Pablo Palma to fill the snake pit with dirt. There were no snakes in it, and I only fell about two feet. I've taken worse falls out of bed."

"Thank God you're alright," Brandon said, as he came to a

stop in front of her. Then he wrapped his arms around her and pulled her gently to him. "So, what are you doing out here in the sticks by yourself? You could get hurt."

"I had to chance it. I was looking for this guy I know."

"Guy? Isn't this a strange place to look for a guy?"

Andrea smiled. "He's a strange guy. So where have you been that it takes a Baker's dozen jaguars to look out for you?"

"I had to try and get rid of that frapping lime green sonofabitch once and for all. There's a Mayan mound about a quarter of a mile from here that's hidden way back in the brush. I took him there."

"Why?"

"Because he 'communicated' to me that the only thing he wanted was to be left alone for the next thousand years or so. All the excavation at the Lost City of the Monkey God is what got him stirred up in the first place. You know...I guess in fifteen hundred years, you kind of get set in your ways."

"So...you just had a friendly chat with that thing?"

"Well, it wasn't exactly like that, but more or less, yeah."

"And now he's gone?"

"I think so. Let's hope so," Brandon said, looking back in the direction he had come from.

"And what about all those jaguars on the trail?" Andrea demanded.

"Friends of Naja," Brandon said with a smile. "Guess they were having the jaguar version of a Tupperware party."

"What happened to being honest?" Andrea asked, returning the smile.

"I am being honest," Brandon said, taking Andrea by the hand and leading her toward the house.

"What? You don't think jaguars are into Tupperware? Besides, I didn't see everything because I fell."

"Stick with me," Andrea said softly, with a loving smile. "I'll keep you from falling."

They had walked no more than a hundred feet when Brandon said, as if it was a fresh idea, "You want honest? Let's get packed," he said. "I want to go to Florida! There's your honest!"

**Don't miss out on your next favorite book!
Join the Melange Books mailing list at**
www.melange-books.com/mail.html

THANK YOU FOR READING

———

Did you enjoy this book?

We invite you to leave a review at your favorite book site, such as Goodreads, Amazon, Barnes & Noble, etc.

DID YOU KNOW THAT LEAVING A REVIEW...

- Helps other readers find books they may enjoy.
- Gives you a chance to let your voice be heard.
- Gives authors recognition for their hard work.
- Doesn't have to be long. A sentence or two about why you liked the book will do.

ABOUT THE AUTHOR

GEORGE DISMUKES spent the first half of his life in pursuit of adventure. This ranged from bullfighting as a youth to milking poisonous snakes professionally at Ross Allen's Reptile Institute in Silver Springs, Florida. The early 60s found him chasing wild animals across the Serengeti in the movie business and operating an animal export company in Iquitos, Peru.

He spent many years exploring archaeological sites of the ancient Maya Indians in Central America and studying their lost civilization. He also lived in Honduras, where the story, TWO FACES OF THE JAGUAR takes place.

In 1980, he began a video production company in Houston, Texas and worked as a 'triple threat' (writer/director/producer) creating some of the Houston market's most creative television commercials. He won a CLEO award for his production of a series of television PSAs concerning prevention of child abuse, funded through a grant from the University of Houston.

Currently, he lives on the Texas Coast with his soul mate and closest friend, Nadine, where he writes and works in magazine advertising.

His hobbies include growing exotic chili peppers and experimenting with salsa recipes. Above all, George is a devout animal lover and has two dogs, named Pulga and Gizmo, respectively.

 twitter.com/dismukes_george